SINCE THE DAY THE MYSTERIOUS COLLIE CALLED KANE HAD COME TO LIVE WITH THEM, THE MCLAUGHLIN FAMILY'S LIFE WAS INDELIBLY CHANGED. Seeming to possess an intelligence and consciousness unlike any dog they had ever known, he became their devoted protector and infallible friend.

To Ben, their young, autistic son, his companionship was essential, but daughter Elizabeth was puzzled by Kane's unwillingness to trust the handsome young man to whom she was attracted.

When the family becomes aware that they are being watched from a distance by strangers unknown and when a family secret is exposed, threatening to split them apart, they learn the importance of the collie's existence in their lives. One dark day a truth is revealed that threatens to tear Kane from the family who loves him, setting off a national frenzy, and drawing him into a daring adventure, one which will challenge Ben to make a crucial decision and a heart-rending sacrifice that will forever affect the special relationship he and Kane have shared, a decision that could endanger the dog he loves.

FOREVER STAY is a story for anyone who has shared the love of a dog and for all who appreciate the special bond and inter-dependency that exists between humans and those magnificent animals.

"Ace Mask knows collies! He uses his innate understanding of the breed to create an emotional and compelling journey through love and loss and love again via a tale of technological terror. Forever Stay is a beautifully crafted boy-and-his-dog adventure for today."

- Jon Provost, actor best known as Timmy from "Lassie."

FOREVER STAY

By ACE MASK

For Donna
who has given me love and collies
and they are the same.

CHAPTER ONE

The pain in Sam Crisp's side, which extended from his neck to the bottom of his feet, was far worse than he had ever experienced and breathing had become increasingly difficult. For the first time in his 78 years of life, he had to consciously force his lungs to inhale and exhale. Sitting on an overstuffed couch in a spacious waiting room outside the executive offices of Prometheacorp, Sam wasn't even sure if he could keep his breathing going long enough to keep his appointment.

Leaning forward slightly, he spoke to the young female receptionist who was busy typing on her desk computer.

"Will it be much longer?" he managed to ask.

The receptionist cast a quick smile in his direction, hardly looking up from her computer screen. "I'm sorry," she said. "Mister Burch has been very busy this morning. He knows you're here. I'm sure he'll be with you momentarily."

Sam nodded wearily and slumped back in his seat. It may have been his labored breathing that eventually prompted her to look at him directly. Suddenly the expression on her face turned to concern as she realized the man before her was not at all well.

"Mister Crisp, are you all right?" she asked.

Sam waved her away but before he could answer, her phone rang, and she picked up the receiver long enough to respond to the caller.

"Yes sir," she said and set the handle back in its cradle.

"Mister Burch can see you now, sir," she said to Sam. "Can I get you a glass of water or . . . ?"

With every effort he could manage, Sam started pulling himself up to a standing position. Seeing his difficulty, the receptionist moved to assist him, and he patted her arm in thanks as he rose.

Motioning to the sofa, Sam told her, "You know, it's possible one could drown in a couch like that. Drown and never found again."

The receptionist managed a smile and took his arm, walking him patiently across the room to a large, heavy door. With effort, she opened it, and Sam patted her arm again as he walked past her, unassisted, into the office.

From behind his desk, a forty-something Tom Burch over-enthusiastically jumped to his feet from an oversized chair and rushed forward to grasp Sam's hand. Like the four other executives seated about the room, he eschewed a suit coat for an immaculately fitted white shirt whose sleeves were rolled up to his elbows to give the impression that he was ready to dive into some kind of work.

"Sam!" Burch gushed. "So good to see you, pal!"

Sam winced slightly at the firm grasp on his hand and forced a slight smile and nod as he looked about the room for an empty chair in which to land.

Still holding his hand, Burch noted his visitor's meek condition.

"Say, are you OK?" he asked, putting his hand on Sam's shoulder and looking into his face with mock concern. With a glance toward the door, which was still held cautiously open by his secretary, he called for her to fetch a glass of water.

"I'll get by I think," Sam managed to say, "if I can just sit down."

"Yeah. Yeah. Right over here, Sam."

An eager executive jumped up and pulled back a seat designated for the guest. Another executive rose from her chair as if to assist and to demonstrate worry and Sam sat down delicately.

The secretary rushed in with a bottle of water, removed the lid and handed the it to Sam who took it with a shaky hand, took a couple of gulps and then handed it back, breathing heavily and sweating profusely.

"This looks serious," Burch said, casting a side-glance to the others in the room. "Why don't you let someone drive you to a doctor?"

An executive who was still standing moved closer to Sam, ready to follow up on the suggestion.

Sam shook his head and when he was able to catch his breath replied, "No. I've been to the doctor. Not much more can be done now."

The ominous response caught Burch by surprise. Regard for the health of the man seated before him was crowded by his concern for something else, and he struggled for a moment with the two priorities.

"Have you . . . have you been working too hard on the Project? Is that what's brought this on?" Burch finally managed to ask. "I heard from some of your staff that you haven't been to the lab for a while."

Sam knew the Project was uppermost in the executive's mind and Sam also knew that concerns about his health existed primarily because Burch knew that if he should die, the formula for the Project would die with him. After a moment, Sam managed enough strength to sit up slightly in his chair.

"That's what I came up here to see you about," Sam said. "The Project is finished."

There was an unconcealed sigh of relief from the others in the room, though it didn't occur to anyone how misplaced that relief was at the moment.

Burch patted Sam on the back before moving back to his chair behind the desk.

"That's great news," he said.

Sam shook his head. "You don't understand. It's finished as far as *you* are concerned. I'm not going to let you have it."

Now Burch was very confused. He looked around the room at the astonished faces, hoping one of them could clarify, squinted his eyes and looked back at Sam. "You're . . . . Wait a minute. We have a contract. You agreed to it. Every minute detail of the project is the absolute property of this organization. *Absolutely.* Remember? You signed a contract, Sam."

The meek gentleman in the guest chair attempted to sit up straight but found he was far too weak. He struggled with his words.

"I'm afraid I'm going to die, Mister Burch. I'm going to die and . . . and I suppose you could say I'm breaking that contract and I'm taking the specs for the Project with me. I won't be turning them over to you. Now you can sue me, but I don't know what good it will do you."

Leaning forward in his chair, Burch was reaching for a life raft. "Your assistants, why they must . . . ."

Sam shook his head. "I distracted them. They provided research, but none of them actually did any work on the real project. Sent them on wild goose chases. Finished the project on my own but, and you need to understand, the more I thought about it, the more I realized this company doesn't deserve to own the rights to this."

"What are you talking about?" Burch sputtered. "Of course we own the rights. We hired you to develop the Project."

Now Sam's breathing became shallow, and he sank deeper in his chair. It was clear he wouldn't be able to speak for long.

"You can't own what you don't have," he said meekly.

Burch pushed his chair back from his desk, unable to mask the look of disbelief on his face.

An executive pulled a cell phone from his lap and began dialing. "I'm calling 9-1-1," he said.

Somehow, Sam was able to pull himself halfway out of his chair, speaking with labored breath. "It's too late for that. I should have left you a note, but I felt I owed it to you to tell you to your face. Now I need to be home. I need to be home with my dog."

His attempt to stand failed, and he fell to the floor. Burch quickly stood, watching from his desk as the others in the room gathered around the fallen man, one of them cradling his head.

"I don't want to die in some hospital," Sam told the man who held him. "I want to be home. With my dog. I need to be with Kane."

"What did he say?" Burch asked. "Who the hell is Kane?"

CHAPTER TWO

Kane stepped out of the low-lying fog that wrapped about the mountain on which he had been wandering, and he stood upon the boulder that jutted out from the mountainside, providing him a full view of the valley below. He lifted his head slightly and sniffed the cool air that drifted past, and he savored the many different aromas that told him so much about the world that surrounded him. The breeze rustled through the collie's thick coat and pushed the clouds back onto the pathway from which he had come.

While Sam was alive, he and Kane had hiked that path daily, enjoying the pacifying sounds of nature, the calming sensation of solitude and peace. As Sam's illness rendered him weak and the walks became more difficult, he was still able to manage the daily ritual almost until the end of his life, somehow strengthened and comforted by Kane and by the sublime sounds of the forest. Their journeys eventually required more frequent pauses for rest as time went on, and Sam would find a boulder or a fallen tree on which to sit, and he would linger until nearly sunset, stroking Kane's head and soft fur as the dog rested his head on his lap, never restless, always contented just to spend time with his god.

Now Sam was gone. He had left one day promising to return, but Kane never saw him again. The loss the dog felt was unlike any pain he had ever known and, afterward, he continued to take the daily walk along the mountain path he had shared with the one living thing he loved most, trying to understand, somehow hoping he would encounter that love again. But he never did. And there was something Sam had given him before he went away, an intelligence and knowledge that no other animal possessed, and that "something" somehow made Sam's absence even harder to bear.

Duty told him he must return before dusk to the home he and Sam had shared in the valley below. Kane knew that Sally, who was looking after the house in Sam's absence, would have a dish of food prepared and waiting for him on the front porch along with a bowl of fresh water and she would be there watching for his return and would open the door for him to enter when he finished his dinner. Though he appreciated Sally's attention, he would soon thereafter retire to the bedroom as he did each evening and climb up on the bed where he could be comforted by the smell the blankets still held of the dear man he missed so intently. Then he would drift off to sleep dreaming that Sam's hand was there, as it always had been, resting upon his head.

Today, however, Kane's senses were telling him something else, something that would again change his life. From the spot where he stood on the mountain he could see the crowded freeway far below and the road that led from it and he could make out a car that was turning off that road onto a smaller road which would end at the entrance to what was, up to this point, the only home he had ever known.

With keen eyesight, he followed the vehicle along its route and eventually, after one last glance over his shoulder at the forest path he had been walking, he slowly moved, though with no sense of urgency, along another path leading down from the mountain that would eventually deliver him back to the house. He was pulled along by an intuition that told him someone needed him. And being needed by someone and being able to serve that someone is the one thing a dog needs most.

CHAPTER THREE

Adults tend to forget how many long periods of boredom one must endure as a child regardless of how many forms of amusement, electronic or otherwise may be at one's fingertips. For Ben at age 9 and in his condition, a long car ride was a monotonous affair difficult to endure. So he sat in the front passenger's seat, resting his head against the car window, staring off into tedium, constantly tapping the fingers of his right hand against the front of his right thigh. For the hour and a half the trip had taken, the rhythm of the tapping never ceased, remaining constant and unvaried.

The destination having nearly been reached, Ben's mother did not let the annoyance of the tapping disturb her. Since it had become a frequent behavior at the age of five, only occasionally did he alter his habit by instead rocking from side to side and the forty-one-year-old schoolteacher had long ago learned to endure what many of lesser patience might have found unendurably aggravating.

Glancing in Ben's direction, she announced, "We're nearly there."

"We're nearly there," he echoed.

"You haven't seen Aunt Sally for quite some time," she reminded him.

"We're nearly there," Ben repeated.

"And I'm told," she said leaning toward him confidentially but not taking her eyes off the road, "I'm told there is going to be a big surprise waiting for you."

"We're nearly there."

The small Northern California town which they had just passed, was surrounded by mountainous terrain through which single lane, generally unpaved roads led to secluded houses, hidden by trees and heavy vegetation. Ben's mother turned the car up one of those roads and the summer sun that shone brightly that afternoon was promptly blocked from view by the heavy foliage overhead.

Ben made no apparent sign of noticing his surroundings, and soon the greenery cleared away, and the filtered light revealed a modest house ahead of them, surrounded by an unpainted wooden picket fence. The shrubbery surrounding the house had been cleared to avoid a fire hazard, and his mother pulled her car up next to an SUV that was parked outside the fence, turned off her engine and looked toward the porch that surrounded the little house.

"Come on, Ben," his mother said as she opened her car door and slid from the driver's seat. Ben stopped tapping his fingers momentarily and began repeatedly nodding his head before gradually opening the door on his side. Once outside the car, he stood next to it, still nodding his head with no intention of going any further.

As his mother approached the front gate, the screen door of the house swung wide, and a wiry, 68-year-old woman called out a warm welcome.

"Afternoon, May! How was the drive?" the woman shouted as she made her way out of the house toward the visitor.

"Hi, Sally," May replied as the two met and shared a friendly hug. "Not bad. We got lucky. Traffic was light."

Sally clutched the younger woman's arms and smiled sweetly into her face. "I appreciate your meeting me here," she told her. "I know I could have brought the dog out to you but, well, I thought it would be a good idea for you to take one last look around your father's place before we clear everything out and put the house up for sale."

May avoided looking into her face and nodded slowly. Sally could plainly see that she wasn't pleased about the visit and was not eager to enter the house as she glanced rather nervously about the yard. Though the yard gave the impression that at one time it may have been very well cared for, flowers suffering from lack of water, ivy and other shrubbery growing unkempt and untrimmed, it now suffered badly from neglect.

Turning her attention away from May, Sally looked toward the car.

"Where's . . . ?" she started to ask but stopped mid-sentence when she spotted Ben still standing by the car, nodding his head, looking off to his right.

Sally patted May's arm and walked toward the boy. Rather than grab him and wrapping him in a warm hug as she so longed to do, she instead held a hand toward him to shake and said gently, "Hello, Ben."

When the boy remained unchanged, she took his hand from his side and started to give it a slight shake, but he promptly pulled his hand back. Sally accepted his reluctance with understanding and patience.

"I haven't seen you for several months. You've grown so much," she said.

She watched Ben for any sign of recognition but seeing none, she tossed her head over her shoulder and suggested to him, "Why don't you come look around the yard? You might find something interesting around here. Go ahead. The yard goes all around the house and let me tell you, the backyard is particularly interesting. There's no telling what you might find back there."

"Come on," she urged him, giving a slight nudge to his arm.

"It's okay," his mother called out to him reassuringly. "Come on, Ben."

After a pause, Ben allowed Sally to lead him into the yard. When the gate was closed behind them she told him, "Now your mother and I are going to go in the house for just a bit so why don't you just look around out here a while?"

She left him and walked past his mother, leading her into the house. Ben remained, his eyes shifting about but never seeming to focus on any one thing. When the screen door closed behind the two adults, he stopped bobbing his head, and his attention focused on a path, which led around the side of the house to the backyard. Whispering something repeatedly to himself, he ventured in that direction.

Inside, scattered about the small front room of the house were piles of books, periodicals, yellow pads containing extensive handwritten notes, large, bulky envelopes and several computer parts, some still unopened in their packages, all in various disorganized stockpiles of disarray. There were large stacks of items apparently designated as trash, and there were various cardboard moving boxes into which some of the room's contents had been carefully placed, identified by descriptions scribbled on the box exteriors with a black marker. Items still to be organized and packed were strewn about the room, perhaps once of some value to the former resident, eventually forgotten and now covered in layers of dust.

Sally paused, hands on hips, and surveyed the scene as May glanced about the room before picking up a book and flipping rather absently through its worn pages.

"Well," Sally said with a weary sigh, "I've been doing my best to get all of this organized and disposed of, but there's still a lot of work to be done. Even as a boy, he couldn't throw anything out no matter how much Mom, and Dad harped at him. 'Course he wouldn't heed my advice about anything either. Who listens to their little sister? Until the day he died, I was always the little sister in his eyes."

Sally shook her head slowly as the two stood among the piles of collected clutter.

May tossed aside the book she held in her hands.

"Even if we had made an effort to come visit him," she mused, "there wouldn't have been any room for us."

Sally frowned. "I don't care what you say or what you think, May. He loved you, a lot more than you think. You don't stop loving an only daughter."

"You don't drop all contact with your only daughter for nineteen years if you love her." She snapped.

"Well . . . ." Sally's voice trailed off with no further defense.

"Come on," she said taking May's arm, "Let's see if we can't find some coffee in the kitchen."

Meanwhile, Ben's attention was temporarily directed toward an old computer terminal, which sat lifeless on a lawn chair in the backyard of the house, and he knelt before it on his knees. Nearby he found a damaged keyboard, and after searching around the back of the machine, he found a spot to insert the plug. The input he used was too large for the object he tried to plug into it, but after jamming the peripheral into the hole several times, he finally managed to make it stay, and he picked up the keyboard and tried to place it on a small space on the chair next to the terminal. The keyboard was too large to lay flat in the open space, so Ben allowed it to rest at an angle, supported on one side by the chair armrest and then proceeded to push one of the keys on the board repeatedly even though there was no response on the dark computer screen.

There was a slight rustle in the thick shrubbery which surrounded the outside of the yard beyond a fifteen-foot clearing, and within the thicket there was the sound of twigs being broken beneath the feet of an animal as it approached. All sound from the brush suddenly stopped, and if one had the keen eyesight of a wild animal, one might have seen a pair of brown eyes peering from within the brush, focused upon the boy in the yard as the creature studied his peculiar actions.

Gradually Ben's hand ceased its repetitious motion at the keyboard, and his body quickly froze, startled by a sudden awareness that he wasn't alone. His eyes darted about the yard, increasingly uneasy. The other pair of eyes watched him curiously from a distance.

Still on his knees and breathing heavily, the boy turned from the keyboard toward the area within the thickness nearby where he sensed the intruder. His eyes danced back and forth over a small area in the thicket.

With a sudden motion, Ben fell backward into a seated position and making a soft, frightened sound he dragged himself, still seated, backward until he was stopped by the bottom step which led from the back door of the house.

In the kitchen, Sally was in the process of pouring two cups of coffee into mugs she had just washed, and she pushed aside various condiments that stacked on the kitchen table, some of which should have been refrigerated long ago. After she and May seated themselves, Sally looked over the table's contents, occasionally picking up a jar and chuckling over the pull date on the label.

"He never really knew how to take care of himself very well after your mother died," Sally mused.

"He certainly wasn't going to ask for my help," said May.

"How is Paul doing?" Sally asked, changing the subject.

It was evident in the way May slouched in her chair that this wasn't a topic she was pleased to discuss.

"Oh, Paul is working himself sick these days, I'm afraid," May said. "He doesn't have much time for the family right now. Spends most of his time in the vineyard. He had to lay off all but a couple of workers, but there's not a lot for them to do. If this damn drought doesn't ease up . . . ."

"How much longer can he hold out?" Sally asked.

May shrugged. "He's probably passed the breaking point already. It's pretty hard for him to give up his dream but he's going to have to do something soon."

The two women continued sipping their coffee in silence for a moment.

"I guess I'm lucky Dad didn't live long enough to see Paul's business go under," May considered. "Paul was the whole reason he shut us out of his life. He said Paul was a dreamer and I deserved better."

Sally nodded. "Your father was cursed with two major afflictions in his life, stubbornness, and genius. He could never accept his inability to control you the way he controlled the computer programs he created but you know, I saw him change these last few months. He closed down the computer lab he was running in town and laid off all the workers and started spending all of his time here, in this house and hiking around in the woods with the dog."

"What was he working on?" May wondered.

Sally shrugged. "Some secret project he'd contracted to do for Prometheacorp, that big pharmaceutical company. He never told me what it was, but I gathered it was something pretty big. Then he closed down the lab and never told the company about it. I think he had a change of heart about the whole project and decided not to finish it."

"He never told you what he was working on? His own sister?" May asked.

Sally shrugged.

"Oh, I almost forgot," Sally said, suddenly standing. "There was something he told me to give you. Something besides the dog."

"Something for me?" May asked, remaining seated.

Sally leaned over and put a hand on her niece's shoulder, smiling. "He thought about you more than you know, my dear. If he'd been given just a bit longer to live, I believe he would have been at your doorstep, asking forgiveness."

May looked doubtful.

"It's in here," Sally said, motioning for her to follow.

Outside, eyes wide, Ben sat unmoving, terrified at something in the brush nearby.

Now the creature could be heard slowly moving closer, the twigs and leaves brushing against its side. Soon it would come into view.

The boy braced himself and opened his mouth widely, preparing to scream.

Clearing the camouflage and stepping into the light there stood before the boy a magnificent, stately collie dog. His thick, deep sable fur shined in the sunlight and contrasted sharply to the gloriously white rough that circled his neck like the mane of a noble lion, accented the markings on all four of his limbs and highlighted the feathering that waved lightly in the breeze like a flag on the back of his front legs.

When fully clear of the thicket in which he had hidden, the dog stood perfectly still, looking toward the boy with an expression combining intelligence and curiosity, his head tilted slightly to one side. His appearance gave not the slightest hint of menace, his entire being radiating a spirit of strength and power and for the first time, Ben's eyes focused directly, though briefly on an object, looking straight into the wonderful animal's face.

Something about the dog gave Ben confidence. He felt his body begin to relax. His mouth, open in anticipation of a scream, slowly closed and his breathing normalized. After several minutes of this curious standoff, a tiny smile began to take shape in the corners of his mouth.

After allowing a few minutes to pass in order for the boy to become more comfortable with his presence, the majestic dog lowered his head in a humble, submissive posture and very slowly stepped toward him. Making his way through a broken spot in the fence, the collie watched the boy's face for any expression of fear but seeing none, he very gradually came closer.

Ben remained rock still. Rather than looking directly at the dog, his eyes appeared to be looking at something immediately beside it, but that was the manner in which he studied things, never looking squarely at the object of his attention but always faintly near it.

Observing the peculiar conduct of the boy, the dog proceeded cautiously and delicately.

Soon the large collie was standing close to him, waiting for a reaction. Seeing none, the dog slowly lay down before him, looking up into his face. He was not insisting on attention, but he was ever so gently persuading the boy to acknowledge him, and in his own quiet and peculiar way, that is exactly what Ben was doing.

The two remained in their respective positions, the boy, curiously studying the creature lying before him and the dog, watching the boy's face for permission and recognition.

In the master bedroom of the house, Sally had just finished working the combination to a small safe that stood against the wall next to a large bed. Kneeling before the safe, she swung wide its door and pulled out the only item inside, a large wooden box. The box seemed a bit heavy, and it was with some difficulty that Sally handed it up to May, who stood next to her.

May looked over the box with very little interest.

"Now what do you suppose he put in there, I wonder?" Sally gasped as she grasped the side of the bed and pulled herself to her feet.

"Documents of some kind," May said, shrugging. "Maybe correspondence."

"Well, there's one way to find out," Sally said, fishing a key from a pocket on the dusty apron she was wearing.

May accepted the key but made no move to unlock the box, picking it up and returning to the kitchen.

"I'll go through it later when we get home," she said over her shoulder.

Back in the kitchen, May dropped the box unceremoniously on the table, tossed the key into her purse and resumed sipping her coffee, staring absently through a window that looked out over the side of the house.

Joining her and picking up her own coffee cup, Sally pondered, "It could be something personal he wanted to share with you. He made me promise to make sure I handed it to you directly."

Wishing to brush aside further discussion of the box' contents but not wishing to hurt Sally's feelings, she smiled at her and replied, "Thank you, Aunt Sally. I'll open it at home. Whatever it is can wait. Is that all he left us, a box and a dog?"

Sally nodded. "Well yes, and the house of course but I'm afraid that when it finally gets sold, we'll barely get enough out of it to pay the back taxes."

"Listen May," she said, "I don't have any idea how important the contents of that box may be, but don't underestimate the importance of the dog."

"Oh, I'm sure it's very important," May said with a smirk, "more important than his family, anyway."

"This is no ordinary animal," Sally said in a very serious tone. "I've been around this dog for some time now, and I've never seen anything quite like him. And don't forget I'm a retired veterinarian."

"What are you talking about?" May asked with concern.

Sally shook her head. "I'm not sure exactly, but I do know he and Sam were very close and I'm pretty sure he and Ben are going to be great friends."

May took a final sip from her coffee cup before walking to the sink and rinsing it off.

"Well," she said, "I welcome any help we can get. He seems to have reached a plateau. When he was younger, one would hardly notice his condition. He could talk your leg off but one day, for who knows what reason, he shut down. I don't know how, but I've got to find a way to flip that switch back on. He's been attending the same school where I teach, and they've been a big help, but now he's out for the summer, and he needs something to keep him busy. "

"What's his prognosis?" Sally asked as May found an old towel and began drying the water off her cup.

"I'm afraid no one knows for sure," May sighed. "There are so many types of autism, and his doesn't seem to match anyone else's symptoms. There's a slim chance he'll improve but then . . . , I don't know. That may just be a mother's optimism."

"You hold on to that optimism," Sally said, giving her a wink. "It's been known to work wonders."

May smiled with appreciation and then looked out a back window, searching for her son.

"I wonder what he's up to back there," she mused. "I'd better check on him."

Sally nodded and set her cup on the sink before opening the kitchen door, which led out onto the back porch. May followed.

The collie lay beside Ben, his head now resting in the boy's lap, looking up into his face. Ben stared straight ahead, his hands placidly at his side. The puzzled expression on his face indicated he didn't understand what he was experiencing.

"Ben, this is Kane," said a gentle, soft voice directly behind him.

Sally was kneeling on the top porch step directly behind him, and May stood behind, looking over her shoulder.

"I think Kane is going to become your new best friend," Sally continued in the same soft voice.

Ben's eyes narrowed almost imperceptibly, and Sally reached around his arm to point directly at the dog.

"Kane," she repeated.

Sally cast a reassuring glance over her shoulder to May, as both waited for the boy's reaction.

After several moments during which it appeared Ben would not respond, he finally whispered, "Kane."

The dog gently wagged his tail.

Kane walked beside the boy all the way to the car. As the car doors were opened, however, the dog stopped and turned around, facing the house. May was too busy buckling Ben's seat belt to notice, but Sally saw Kane slowly walk back toward the front porch and push on the screen door with his foot as he had done so many times throughout his life. The door bounced open far enough for him to push it open with his muzzle. Sally knew his intention as the door swung open wide enough for him to enter and pass through.

"Where's the dog?" May asked as she glanced around the yard.

"He'll be back in a moment," Sally assured her knowingly.

Kane walked through the cluttered front room of the house and into the bedroom. He paused for a moment, looking forlornly at the bed he had shared for so long with his best friend. Gradually he walked to the bed and lifted his front paws up to its edge, resting his head between them. He gazed tenderly toward the pillow for several moments and then with a deep sigh, he removed his feet and slowly walked out of the room toward a new life.

Crossing the front porch, Kane paused to sniff the air and look off into the distance. He couldn't see it from where he stood, but he somehow knew a dark-colored car was parked on the shoulder where the road intersected the main highway. He had seen it there earlier that day as he returned home from his walk in the hills. It had remained parked there for most of the day, and though Kane didn't know who was inside, he sensed that the house was being watched and an involuntary growl, barely audible, formed in his throat.

"Kane?" called Sally from the yard. "Come along, boy. Everything will be fine here, I promise."

Kane approached the car like a soldier stepping cautiously across a minefield. Something was wrong. Sally could see that plainly enough. But what?

As the car pulled away from the house, she could see Kane, sitting in the back seat, looking at her through the closed window and she thought to herself, "He's telling me to be careful."

A minute later, the car was pulling out on to the main road, and Kane could see that the dark-colored car was still parked on the shoulder.

The collie's low growl resumed.

CHAPTER FOUR

As May navigated her car homeward, she occasionally glanced at Ben in the passenger's seat next to her. She had tried to persuade him to join Kane in the back seat, but Ben would have no part of it. The front seat was where he always sat, and that was where he insisted he sit now. Although he was still tapping incessantly on his leg with his fingers, he would occasionally stop for a minute or two, looking out the window at the passing scenery, his mind buried deep in thought. Eventually, he would resume his habit, but this was a deviation of his behavior, however small, and she made a mental note to be sure to share this observation with his doctor on his next scheduled visit.

Looking in the car's rearview mirror, she could see the dog lying across the seat, his head down. He didn't sleep, and his eyes stared blankly before him. She thought he appeared depressed but then gave him no further thought.

Sally had provided dog bowls and enough kibble to last Kane a couple of weeks but May decided to pick up a bag to have on hand should the supply run low. On the way home, she drove to a small section of town and parked her car in one of the perpendicular parking spaces in front of a small feed store she occasionally frequented.

She rolled down all of the windows and explained to Ben that she was going into the store for a moment and asked him to wait in the car with Kane. She knew better than to ask Ben if he would like to accompany her because she knew that his response would be a strong negative.

May paused a moment, watching her son as he stared out the window, tapping his fingers. Kane looked up at her as she turned her head to address him in the back seat.

"Kane," she said, "Keep an eye on Ben. OK, boy?"

Somehow, the look on the dog's face reassured her that he would do that very thing. She smiled at him and then opened the car door, but before she moved out of her seat, she stopped. Thinking on the non-verbal response she had just received from her request, she looked back at Kane again.

"You understand, don't you?" she asked, but it was more of a statement than a question.

Kane stared blankly back at her, and after looking into his eyes for a moment, she turned and stepped out of the car, thinking to herself, "I actually think he does."

The dog watched her as she entered the feed store then he turned his attention back to Ben, whose actions were unchanged, and the boy seemed not even to notice that his mother had left. Thus reassured, Kane lay his head down between his paws.

After several minutes, he became aware of a loud, deep, pounding sound nearby. Eyes suddenly wide, he sat up quickly in the center of the seat, and after a quick survey of the area, he spotted the source of his unease.

In the front seat of a brightly polished black sedan parked three spaces away, two young men known to local law enforcement as the Keegan brothers reclined as they guzzled beer in thirsty gulps while a persistent booming bass blasted from the car's shabby, overworked speakers. Mitch, the younger of the two boys, an immature beard doing its best to take root on his blemished skin, the hair on his head trimmed in a buzz-cut, slouched behind the steering wheel, alternating between gulps of beer and puffs from a cigarette. His brother Conrad, older by two years, festooned with poorly designed tattoos, wore his greasy hair shoulder length and was resting one leg out the open front passenger's side window. The door on his side of the vehicle was badly dented, and all of the car's windows were tinted much darker than was permitted by law.

It would have been an accurate judgment of character to conclude that neither individual was honestly employed and, in fact, Conrad was presently taking stock of a nearby liquor store's surveillance cameras with an eye toward a future burglary.

Tossing an empty can into the gutter by his car, Conrad was about to reach for another beer on the seat between them when his eye caught sight of Ben.

"Hey," he said to his brother, nodding toward the boy.

"Yeah," acknowledged Mitch.

"We seen him around town before, remember? That retard?" Conrad reminded him.

"Sure, we know that guy," Mitch confirmed. Recognizing the mischief that his brother was devising, he attempted to divert his attention. "Say, why don't we go see what Danny and Billy are doin'?"

"Later," Conrad replied. "Let's go say 'hi' to the retard first."

With a high-pitched laugh, he reached for a baseball bat, which he kept under the seat. It was an instrument that enjoyed a great many applications, none of them sporting. In fact, its primary use was for knocking rural mailboxes from their posts very late at night as the two brothers raced down local roads on the outskirts of town, Mitch behind the wheel while Conrad brandished the bat. Though many locals suspected the two boys to be the authors of the mischief, they'd never been caught in the act. Aside from that, Conrad also found the bat to be useful for breaking windows from time to time while Mitch kept a lookout for witnesses. Though the younger brother recognized Conrad's tendency toward illegal high jinks, he felt a deep sense of loyalty to him. Neither brother had successfully held a job for any length of time, so Mitch relied on Conrad to "provide," illegally or otherwise.

Conrad threw his body heavily against the damaged car door, and after two attempts, it swung noisily open. He continued his giggling and swung the bat at his side as he approached Ben's car, while Mitch followed a few steps behind.

Watching the brothers approach, Kane backed himself away from the window and sat quietly, unseen by the two of them as he observed their actions.

Conrad noisily tapped the door next to Ben with his bat. "Hey there, retard! How's it going?" he greeted the boy.

Ben stopped tapping his fingers but did not stare directly at them.

Mitch slapped the side of his brother's shoulder. "Oh, come on, Conrad. That's not a nice thing to call somebody like him. You better not let anybody hear you call him that."

"Yeah, what was I thinkin'?" Conrad said, slapping his forehead. "I guess maybe I'm the retard, huh? Man, I'm sorry for callin' you a retard, OK, retard?"

Studying Ben for a moment, he lit a cigarette, considering the next step in his harassment game.

"Hey!" he exclaimed. "Whyn't ya let me make it up to ya? Come over here on the sidewalk a minute. Let's have some fun." Backing up a few steps, he banged on the pavement with his bat to indicate where he wanted Ben to stand.

The boy cast a quick glance at the bat but didn't move.

"Come on!" coaxed Conrad.

At this point Kane, who had been sitting in the back seat unnoticed by the brothers, now showed himself, moving swiftly to the window.

At the sudden appearance of the dog, Mitch moved quickly backward several steps, but Conrad failed to notice the intrusion as he opened Ben's door.

"What?" asked Conrad, as he noticed his brother's startled reaction. Following the direction of Mitch's attention, Conrad finally noticed the dog who was now intently staring into his eyes.

"Whoa!" the bully said, putting some distance between himself and Kane. "Where did *that* come from?"

The brothers stood a safe distance from the car, uncertain as to the danger in which they may have placed themselves.

"Hey retard," Conrad called out to Ben, pointing to Kane with his cigarette. "Does your dog bite?"

Ben did not respond but stepped out of the car and stood in the spot on the sidewalk where he had been invited.

"That's right," Conrad said with a nervous laugh, watching the collie from the side of his eye. Feeling a bit braver because the dog had not made a move on him, he motioned Ben to come closer and placed an arm around his shoulder while Mitch watched nearby.

"Now," Conrad continued, brandishing the bat before Ben. "We're gonna play a game of 'T' ball. You ever done that? Played 'T' ball? Let's see. What can I use?"

While he looked around for something he could use in his game, he spotted his discarded beer can in the gutter and called out to Mitch to toss it to him.

"Careful now, Conrad," Mitch warned as he picked up the can. Calling out to Ben to catch, he tossed it lightly to him, but the boy was unprepared for the pitch, and the can bounced off his chest to the pavement.

"Now, that's the very thing right there!" Conrad exclaimed as he snatched the can and flipped it up and down in his hand a few times. "The very thing. OK, you just stand very, very still, you got me? It'll be fun."

Carefully balancing the beer can on Ben's head, he took two steps back and prepared to swing the stick toward it.

"Nah, that's too easy," he said after several slow practice swings. Removing the can from Ben's head, he stood it upright on the sidewalk and with a swift move, slammed it violently with the bat, smashing it flat. Picking up the crushed can, he replaced it back on the boy's head.

"Yeah," Conrad said, standing back to watch the fun, "that's more fair. Now, don't you move any ' cause I don't want to smash your head off too bad, OK?"

"Hey, come on," Mitch said. "You had a couple of beers, maybe we oughta . . . ."

"Nah, I won't hurt nothin'," reassured Conrad. "If I bust his head, there won't be no brains oozin' out or nothin'."

Mitch reluctantly joined his brother in laughter at the remark, and Conrad tossed aside his cigarette as he held the bat in preparation for a swing at the flattened object. Ben just watched, uncertain, but curious.

It was at that moment that Kane appeared, inserting himself sideways between the batter and the boy. He had jumped unseen and unheard from the open car window and now assumed a protective position, startling Conrad, who lowered his bat and moved backward.

"What the . . . ?" he muttered under his breath as the dog turned his head and looked up into his face. The look in the collie's eyes was not overtly threatening, but it was sufficient to telegraph to Conrad that this game was now at an end.

Grabbing his bat with both hands, Conrad held it aggressively high, ready to divert his swing at the dog's skull but Kane's gaze was not distracted, and for a moment dog and troublemaker were locked in a frozen showdown.

"You know, if the retard don't want to have no fun," Mitch finally interposed, "that's his tough luck. Let's go. We can make friends with that flea-bag friend of his at a later time. What say, Conrad?"

For several seconds more Conrad wrestled with the decision to strike or hike before Kane's unwavering stare convinced him to lower his bat.

"Yeah," he said. "Stupid mutt. I won't waste no time on him. Anyway, I need another beer." Stopping at the car, he turned back toward Kane and pointed at him with the bat. "You and me are gonna meet up again someday, dog, and we'll pick up where we left off."

As the two men got back into their car, May exited the feed store, followed by a young female clerk who carried a large bag of kibble. May had come upon the scene just in time to see

Conrad's surrender, and though she hadn't witnessed what preceded that point, there was little doubt in her mind that a threat to her son had just been averted.

"Ben!" she called, taking his arm with one hand and removing the smashed can from the top of his head with the other as she knelt beside him. "What are you doing out of the car?"

The boy made a loud sound and immediately pulled his arm away from her, and as this occurred, the Keegan brothers raced noisily by, revving their car engine as they tossed another empty beer can into the street.

"Retard!" Conrad yelled out the window as they sped down the street, laughing raucously.

May became aware that Kane was watching her, his ears back against his head, a reassuring look upon his face. She studied his expression for several moments before returning to her car.

On the ride home, May couldn't stop thinking about the dog in the back seat, and she couldn't stop wondering what his addition to their family would mean.

CHAPTER FIVE

The vintage two-story house Kane would now call home was set a short distance from the highway. Surrounded by a wire fence framed in wood, it was comfortably nestled among fields of dry grape vines and large, rolling hills and age-worn oak trees. Next to the driveway entrance, a modest sign carved in wood identified the location as "McLaughlin Vineyards."

May pulled her car up next to a blue pick-up truck which displayed a replica of that same sign upon its door. As she did so, she could see Chuck and Ray, two of her husband's three employees, conversing as they leaned against a tractor that stood idly in front of the large barn-like building that doubled as a winery and product warehouse. The ivy that climbed the side of the building, like much of the vegetation in the area, was varying shades of brown and gray.

May smiled and waved casually at the two men as she stepped from her car and opened the car trunk to get the bag of kibble. Among the dog bowls and supplies provided by Sally was her father's box which Sally had placed there before leaving. May made a mental note to retrieve it later.

She called out to Ben as he slid from the car seat and shut the door.

"Why don't you take Kane and introduce him to your dad?"

Ben hesitated a moment, a slight frown on his face as he considered his mother's suggestion before opening the door to allow the dog to exit.

Walking into the house with the bag of dog food under her arm, she called back to him, "Don't let Kane wander too far from the house. He doesn't know his way around here yet. We don't want him to get lost."

It wasn't apparent whether Ben understood his mother's words as he stood staring into the vineyards. Kane watched May as the front door closed behind her and then took one step toward the fields, surveying the area before looking back into the boy's face. The look prompted Ben to comply with his mother's request, and he walked toward the winery as Kane followed.

Ben wandered aimlessly among the hefty wooden casks and stainless steel wine processing equipment sitting within the large, dimly lit building as the collie walked at his side, exploring and occasionally sniffing this strange new world. The sound of two men engaged in a quiet conversation eventually led them to the boy's father, leaning against a piece of machinery with a piece of paper in his hand. Andrew, who was in charge of overseeing his business operation, was staring at the floor as the two conversed in hushed tones.

Andrew nodded his head, signaling to the boy's father of his approach. His father, absorbed in conversation, cast a quick glance at his son without appearing to see him and resumed his talk, making no acknowledgment of the dog at his side.

As the two men conversed, Ben idly pulled the paper from his father's hand. He waved it through the air for a moment before his father snatched it back without even looking. While the talk continued, Ben tried to retrieve the paper, but his father held it up high enough that he couldn't reach it.

The boy continued to try to grasp the object but, having no success, he began to vocalize with small grunts of frustration which became increasingly louder as he stretched his arm upward and he began jumping in a useless attempt to grab it. Although his father didn't allow this irritation to disrupt his conference, his annoyance at the boy's disturbance increased as Ben jumped higher and with greater exaggeration and the sounds he was making became short, piercing squeals.

At a point his father could bear no more, Kane suddenly stepped forward and placed his body between the two of them. Surprised, Ben stood for a moment staring blankly ahead before the dog nudged the boy's chest with his muzzle, causing him to take a step back. The boy stood silently, uncomprehending.

Though Ben's father continued to speak without noticing what had just taken place, Andrew stared down at the dog in amazement.

"Did you just see that?" Andrew asked, interrupting.

"Hmm?" asked Ben's father, looking down at his son blankly.

"What happened just now with 'Lassie' there," said Andrew pointing to the dog and the boy who stood silently by him. "How did that dog know to do that?"

The boy's father was not to be distracted, however.

"I'll tell you what," he said, resuming the topic at hand. "Let's just sleep on it a couple of days and let me figure out where we go from here. I'll talk to you Wednesday, OK?"

Andrew took the man's extended hand and shook it then nodded to the boy and walked toward the door. When he was several feet away, he stopped, looked back at Ben and the dog before resuming his exit, shaking his head.

Ben's father stood staring at the spot where Andrew had just stood, and after a moment of contemplation, he turned to leave, placing his hand on the boy's shoulder to invite him to walk with him. Ben walked beside his father but brushed his hand away from his shoulder with a verbal grunt. Kane followed them as they walked toward the house.

As Ben's father, looking weary and burdened with responsibility, trudged up the few steps that led to the front porch, the boy detoured and walked deliberately into the vineyard at the side of the house. Not noticing, his father entered the front parlor and allowed the screen door to slam shut behind him.

Kane at first stood watching the front door before turning to see Ben disappear down a row of lifeless grape vines. The dog trotted after the boy.

Inside the front parlor, Ben's father sank into a comfortable armchair with a long sigh and massaged his closed eyes with his fingers. Having heard the door close, May found Paul in this position, and after studying him for a moment, she sat on the couch facing him, waiting for him to speak.

When he didn't acknowledge her, she called out to him.

"Paul?" she called.

Eventually, drained and dispirited, he dropped his hand from his eyes and squinting at the sunlight streaming through the window, he was able to speak in a weary, hollow voice.

"I guess it's all finally over, May," he said.

"What does Andrew think?" she asked.

Paul shrugged. "We'll have to start looking for a buyer, but I don't know who's going to spend any money as long as this drought hangs on."

Unable to face his wife, he looked around the room awhile before speaking again. "I'll talk to Bob Simmons about any job prospects. There won't be any money coming in from this place, but maybe we can hold on to the property for a while if I can land a job that will pay enough. I don't suppose we'll see any money from the sale of your father's house?"

May shook her head. She tried hard to think of something to say that would lift his spirits before suddenly remembering the drive home.

"Did Ben introduce you to Kane?" she asked in a brighter tone.

Paul tried to pull himself back from the cave where his thoughts had retreated.

"Who?" he asked.

Suddenly May stood, as a worried realization started to sweep over her.

"The dog," she said. "I told Ben to find you and show you the dog. Didn't you see him?"

Now Paul sat up straight, quickly understanding May's concern.

"Yeah, but . . . ." Paul was trying to remember where Ben had gone after they left the barn.

May rushed to the door and exclaimed swiftly under her breath, "I hope he hasn't wandered off."

Paul jumped up from his chair, swearing at himself for his carelessness as he rushed out behind her.

Outside, they both began calling his name, unsure which way to begin searching.

"I'll check the warehouse," Paul said, rushing toward the building. His voice could be heard echoing inside the large structure as he called for Ben.

May rushed to one side of the house, calling her boy's name desperately down the furrows of grape vines, then returned, rushing toward a field on the opposite side as her panic began to build.

At length Paul and May met back in front of the house, both of them panting frantically.

"He's not in the warehouse," Paul gasped. "You look in the north field, and I'll look over here."

May nodded and started off before suddenly stopping.

"Ben!" yelled out Paul as he started off toward the field.

"Wait!" May yelled, standing very still.

Faintly, in the distance beyond the fields, she could hear the far-off sound of a dog barking.

Suddenly May screamed to her husband as she ran toward the source of the sound. "The reservoir! He can't swim!"

It took Paul but a moment for her words to penetrate before he took off after her, quickly closing the distance between them and nearly stepping on her heels as they scrambled between rows of vines that ascended and then descended first one rolling hill and then another. The distance and the time it was taking to reach their Ben seemed infinite as they raced, gasping for breath, their hearts pounding with fear and exertion.

May only thought of grabbing Ben and pulling him back from the danger the water in the open reservoir held for him if he fell in. How long had he been missing? Might they be too late? Didn't Paul say yesterday the reservoir had been filled possibly for the last time because of limits imposed by the drought? In that case, it could be full. These thoughts and others wove swiftly through an intense feeling of dread she felt as she tore her way forward.

With no sense of the time it had taken them to reach their destination, Paul and May were soon clambering up the dirt berm that surrounded the man-made reservoir at the edge of their property, and they stopped only for a moment before spotting Ben standing atop the opposite bank. Resuming their sprint to reach him, they rushed to his location, finally slowing their pace as they came nearer, covering the remaining distance between them at a swift walk, panting to catch their breath.

"Ben!" May gasped as Paul came to a halt next to her. "I've told you, never, *ever* come here without . . . ."

She stopped. Having been so panicked and oblivious to anything except the sight of her son standing unharmed she failed to notice what he had been doing and she hadn't noticed the dog. Forgetting for a moment the fierce fight her lungs were waging for more air, she unconsciously held her breath and observed in wonderment the activity before her.

Kane stood sideways in front of Ben, blocking him from entering the water. The boy was idly pushing against the dog repeatedly to move out of the way, but Kane's legs were locked, and though Ben would sometimes push against him with enough strength to cause him to lose his footing temporarily, he would immediately restore his position, firm and unyielding.

As remarkable as May found Kane's action to be, at the same time she felt an uncanny sensation wash over her. Slowly she reached for Ben's shoulder and guided him back toward the house, her gaze locked on the path before her, attempting to understand what she had just seen.

Paul remained behind a moment, with the dog, seeing him for the first time. Kane was watching May and Ben as they walked away then shifted his attention to Paul. His tail wagged slowly.

Reaching out, Paul slowly stroked the dog's head, unable to find words to thank the dog who stood before him.

Kane stepped away from him and trotted after May and Ben.

CHAPTER SIX

Over dinner that evening, May told Paul about Kane's actions in protecting Ben from the bullies in town earlier that day, and the two of them asked each other questions about the dog that neither of them could answer. Were his actions protecting Ben instinctive? Did Sam teach Kane this behavior? Was the dog exceptionally intelligent? Well, they both agreed that the last question answered itself. They had never known a more intelligent dog.

While they talked, Ben played with his food, managing to eat a bit of it from time to time while Kane, having finished his dinner, lay on the floor beside him oblivious to the conversation taking place. Earlier he had been allowed to explore the house, and he had inspected each room, upstairs and down, familiarizing himself with the many aromas that identified every item of clothing, each shoe and boot and every item in every closet. Only after he had contented himself that he had classified and cataloged every fragrance did he consent to eating his dinner.

Now, at Ben's side, the dog lifted his head as he heard a car pull up in front of the house and shut off its motor. No one at the dinner table noticed as he rose to his feet and walked from the dining room to the front door. Looking through the screen, he observed a young girl, about 19, as she closed her car door and walked toward the house.

At the door, she stopped, surprised to see the collie surveying her from inside.

"Well hello there," she greeted him cheerfully. "Aren't you a beauty?"

She opened the door, and Kane stood back to allow her to pass. She paused to gently tousle the white rough around his neck as she looked into his brown eyes, so intelligent and wise.

"Yeah," she said under her breath. "A real beauty."

Kane followed her into the dining room where Paul and May warmly embraced their daughter.

"Hi, Elizabeth," Ben intoned quietly, repeating his parents' greeting as he played with the food on his plate.

His sister turned to him and seated herself at the table where a place had been set for her next to her brother. She gave him a hug and a kiss on the cheek as May dished food onto her daughter's plate.

"I'm home for the whole summer, Ben. We'll have lots of time to spend together," Elizabeth said to him. "Well, most of the summer, anyway, when I'm not working."

Kane laid himself back down next to Ben and watched her as she spoke.

"Sally will be doing some part-time work in the veterinary clinic where she used to work," Elizabeth continued. "She's going to mentor me and allow me to assist her."

Her parents nodded their approval.

"You'll be learning from the best," May confirmed.

"Found any good looking up and coming veterinary students over there at UC Davis?" her father teased.

"Sorry to disappoint you, Pop," Elizabeth replied, smiling. "I've been too busy studying to notice."

"Sure you have," Paul said, winking at his wife.

May was grateful that he could smile and enjoy himself for a while before his thoughts pulled him back into depression.

"But who is the gorgeous new family member?" Elizabeth asked, pointing to the dog.

"This gentleman is named Kane," her mother told her. "He's your little brother's self-appointed protector."

May related the circumstances surrounding the coming of the collie to the McLaughlin Family and of the surprising episodes that had taken place that day.

Elizabeth turned and looked earnestly at the dog who sat studying her every move.

"Well, collies do have a reputation for being great with kids," said Elizabeth. "And you know, 'Lassie' and all that. They were once used to herd and take care of sheep. Maybe Kane thinks Ben is a little lamb."

"Is that what you are, Ben?" she teased, giving her brother a slight nudge on his arm. "Are you our little lamb?"

Ben rested his head on his hand as he chewed on a piece of beef much longer than was actually necessary.

"Well, you're a handsome devil, Mister Kane," Elizabeth said, looking back at the dog and giving him a scratch behind the ear. "And a hero to boot. How about you be my boyfriend for the summer? I don't think I could do any better."

After dinner, and after the dishes had been cleaned and put away, they relaxed in the front room of the house, Ben seated on the floor as he scribbled abstract images on a sheet of art paper with a crayon. He always used a blue crayon to create his unusual illustrations, leaving the rest of the crayons untouched in the box that held them.

Paul sadly explained to his daughter the demise of his dream and that he would have to start looking for a job in order to continue supporting the family. Elizabeth offered to quit school and move back home and get a job to help out, but Paul and May would hear nothing of it. Nothing was more important, they emphasized, than for her to finish her education so that she could someday realize her ambition to become a veterinarian.

Kane, resting on the floor not far from Ben, gradually felt a discomfort overtake him. Lifting his head, he tried to interpret an unseen signal, sensing that *something* wasn't right.

He studied the screen door for a moment before rising and walking toward it. May noticed him looking through the screen and interpreted it to mean he needed to go outside. Rising from the couch, she crossed to the door and opened it, allowing the dog to pass. As she closed the door behind him, she admonished him to stay close to the house and watched him for a moment before returning to the couch.

"He won't run away or get lost out there, will he?" Elizabeth asked.

"Not that dog," May replied with confidence.

It was dusk as Kane stood at the bottom of the front stair, peering into the distance as the last vestiges of sunlight disappeared beneath the horizon. The premonition that something was not what it should be pulled him toward the road that led past the house.

As he approached the road, he spotted the source of his uneasiness. Driving very slowly past the house was the same dark car he had seen parked that morning near his former home. Now it conveyed the same ominous portent. The driver, unseen because of darkly tinted windows appeared to be surveying the house as the car inched along.

His body tense and his head held low with apprehension, Kane crept toward the road in a crouched position, watching as the vehicle drove by. When it had passed the house some distance down the road, the car suddenly accelerated and disappeared rapidly from sight down the highway.

For over an hour Kane sat at the entrance to his new home as darkness overtook the landscape, his attention focused in the direction the disquieting automobile had traveled.

CHAPTER SEVEN

At bedtime, Kane was shown a plush dog-sized mattress that had been placed beside Ben's bed in the boy's room in an upper floor of the house. The collie was indifferent to such comfort and instead jumped up on the bed, finding the perfect sleeping spot beside Ben's feet. Kane looked up at May as she tucked her son into bed, not with an expression that begged permission to sleep in that location but rather one that simply made the statement that his proper place was right there, with the boy.

"Oh, no you don't," May admonished the dog. "You'll get hair and dirt on the blankets. You've got a perfectly good spot to sleep right over there on the floor."

But Paul happened to be walking down the hallway that led past Ben's room at that moment and called to May as he passed.

"Let him sleep on the bed," Paul commanded. "He's earned it I'd say."

Looking at the dog, May sighed a breath of resignation as Paul's footsteps continued down the hallway.

"All right," she said under her breath, addressing Kane. "I guess there's too many other things to worry about right now. But if Ben wets the bed tonight, you're going to wish you heeded my advice."

She leaned over her son and placed a kiss on his forehead then chuckled to herself as she walked toward the switch by the door and turned off the lights. She knew Ben had not wet the bed in some time.

A dim ray of light cast itself through the doorway, allowing May to take one last goodnight look at the vision of her son as he lay on his back looking earnestly at the ceiling, continually whispering something repeatedly under his breath.

The dog remained alert, looking into her face with an expression that bestowed to her a feeling of comfort and safety and thus soothed, she pulled the door to, leaving it open but a crack.

It was a new sentiment Kane was experiencing. Instead of falling to sleep with Sam's comforting hand on his head, conveying a feeling of sublime peace, the collie had now tasked himself to impart the same serenity to the young boy who was soon breathing the peaceful breath of sleep.

Inching himself closer to Ben's side, Kane managed to nudge his head under the boy's hand. The two would remain in that position all night.

CHAPTER EIGHT

Sam's funeral was to be a simple graveside affair, and even that much ceremony was strictly against his wishes. When his illness grew worse, and he grasped the fact that his final days were near he had instructed Sally to have his body cremated after death and to spread the ashes along the mountain trail, he and Kane frequented daily. Sally would hear nothing of it.

"Look," she told him. "Since you don't have a dime to put toward funeral arrangements, I'll be the one paying to have you buried, so you don't have any say in the matter."

"Far as I'm concerned," Sam retorted, "you can throw my remains in a ditch and kick some dirt over 'em. But whatever you do, *no service!*"

After Sam died, Sally made up her mind that a minimal graveside service would be an adequate compromise between Sam's wishes and her own. She thought if he had lived long enough she would have talked him into it anyway.

On the day of the funeral, the McLaughlin family was gathered and herded toward their car for the trip to the cemetery. They were surprised that an unexpected mourner had decided to join them and he had already planted himself in the middle of the back seat.

"Out," May ordered him with a firm gesture.

Kane remained seated.

"Come on, Kane, OUT!" May commanded again.

Kane laid himself down.

Paul studied the dog for a moment before putting his hand on May's shoulder.

"Wait," he told her. "He looks like he knows where we're going and if anyone has a right to be there today, it's Kane."

"But he can't . . . ." May struggled, "How can he know where we're going? They won't let a dog into the cemetery. He can't go with us."

While May ticked off a list of reasons why Kane couldn't go, the rest of the family silently filed past her into the car seating themselves in their respective places, long ago assigned by family tradition. Ben and Elizabeth sat in the back seat with Kane between them while their father slid behind the steering wheel.

Leaning across the front seat, Paul called out to May through the open passenger side door.

"Going with us?" he asked.

Shaking her head and throwing her hands into the air in a gesture of frustration, she gave up and took a seat next to him. Casting a glance over her shoulder, she observed Elizabeth giving a hug to Kane as she smiled playfully. She also noticed that Ben's head was turned in the direction of the dog and that there was a slight smile on his face. What delighted her particularly was the fact that his hands were perfectly still. No tapping.

The drive to the cemetery was relatively brief. Sally had selected the location of Sam's final resting place next to his long deceased wife's plot which was, conveniently, situated not far from the residence of his oldest daughter. Sally would never give up hope that May would someday make an occasional visit to her father.

Paul steered his car into the cemetery entrance and waited behind a string of three or four cars which were, one by one, pausing by the guard shack to be directed by the security guard on duty to the location of the service they were attending. Not far from the entrance stood a large chapel in front of which a large number of cars were parked. Paul knew that the crowd of mourners lined up in front of his car, as well as several that took their place in line behind him, were not headed to Sam's funeral. He wasn't likely to have that many friends show up.

Gradually the McLaughlin family car reached the guard shack, and a smartly uniformed guard stepped from his duty post to greet the new collection of visiting mourners.

"Name of deceased?" the guard asked with a military demeanor.

"Crisp," Paul replied, sharing a brief smile with May at the abruptness of the question.

Quickly stepping into his station, the guard grabbed a small map and circled a spot signifying the location of the service for Sam Crisp. Handing the map to Paul, he provided verbal directions specifying each turn to the destination with precise gestures before snapping into a position of attention far more suited to an army base than a memorial park.

Paul thanked him and started his car in the direction he had been instructed, but as the rear passenger window passed by him, the guard suddenly called out to Paul.

"Hold on!" the guard yelled, stepping over to the car window.

"Is that a dog, sir?" the guard asked, pointing to the back seat.

Paul wondered if he really was expecting an answer to what would have seemed a rhetorical question.

Glancing over his shoulder at Kane, Paul replied slowly, "Why, yes. I believe it is."

The guard shook his head firmly. "I'm very sorry, sir," the guard said. "Dogs are specifically prohibited on these premises. Only trained guide dogs allowed. So unless that's a trained guide dog, you'll need to pull forward and make a U-turn back toward the exit here."

"Look," Paul began, "I understand the reason for the rule, but we were hoping you could make a special exception. You see . . . ."

Before Paul could continue, the driver of the car immediately behind the McLaughlins called out.

"Excuse me!" yelled the driver impatiently.

Looking in the driver's direction, the guard was alarmed to see that a long line of cars had suddenly formed at the entrance and he rushed back toward his post with haste quickly losing his military bearing.

"Far be it from me to say anything like, 'I told you so,'" May said to Paul with eyebrows raised. "You'd better move the car, dear. You're going to make all those people late back there." She nodded toward the ever-increasing queue behind them.

After a momentary pause, Paul accelerated but rather than make a U-turn as instructed, he guided the car forward in the direction of the Crisp service. Glancing in his rearview mirror, he confirmed that the guard was far too preoccupied with the other cars to notice. Elizabeth laughed, and May shook her head with resignation.

A small group of mourners had already assembled around Sam Crisp's gravesite by the time the McLaughlin family arrived and parked their car. A number of May's and Paul's friends joined them, and May recognized most of the other attendees as friends of Sally. She doubted that many of those present were even acquainted with her father though she admitted to herself that she didn't know everyone who had gathered.

Sally stepped forward from beneath the canvas awning which covered the gravesite to greet the family warmly, providing well wishes and big hugs all around.

"You brought Kane!" she exclaimed with delight as she saw the dog walking beside Ben. "If anyone has a right to be here today, it's him."

May pretended not to notice Paul's self-satisfied smirk and thanked her aunt for having made all of the funeral arrangements. She surveyed the simple urn set atop a draped pedestal centered beneath a portable canopy and noted with surprise a conspicuously large floral display prominently placed nearby.

"From the management of Prometheacorp," Sally said. "I think that's their way of appeasing their guilt for not having sent anyone to the funeral. Pretty ostentatious. I don't think Sam would approve."

While they spoke, Ben became aware that Kane was no longer at his side. He quickly spotted him sitting unnoticed in front of the white folding chairs that had been set in rows for the guests. Kane lay before the urn, contemplating it with a mournful expression on his face. Ben joined his dog and stood beside him, looking curiously at the object of his dog's attention.

"Listen," Sally said to May and Paul conspiratorially, not noticing the unusual sight of the boy and dog nearby. "There's something I need to tell you. I've sensed that something has been going on around your father's place and yesterday I received a phone call . . . ."

At that moment a man dressed in blue jeans and sport coat called out, "Ladies and gentlemen. If you will all be kind enough to take your seats, perhaps we can begin."

Sally patted May's arm. "I'll tell you later," she said to her.

It was at that moment and at the same time that May and her aunt noticed with some surprise that Ben was staring at the urn. Joining him, his mother leaned in to his ear and asked him to sit beside her in a seat in the first row of chairs.

The boy at first followed obediently, but when he noticed that the dog had not joined him, Ben pulled away from his mother and rushed back to sit on the ground beside Kane. May called out for Ben to return to her.

"Why not just let him be," Sally suggested, and after considering for a moment, May agreed.

The young man in jeans and sport coat conducted a relatively brief, non-denominational service before asking the guests if anyone would like to say a few words about the departed. Sally was the first to volunteer, reminiscing about their shared childhood and eliciting a few chuckles as she related incidents that illustrated Sam's cantankerous nature. She concluded by stating her firm belief that in spite of his estrangement from his daughter and her family, he truly loved them as evidenced by the fact that his final act was to bequeath his most cherished possession to his grandson. She nodded to

Kane, lying before her with his head on the ground between his front paws.

"Ben here has a large obstacle to overcome as he matures," she said, "but judging from the friendship he's already formed with his new dog, I'd say he has an important companion to help guide him along his way."

Observing the focus of Ben's attention, Sally approached Sam's urn and lifted it, cradling it in her arms. Smiling at those seated before her, she continued.

"I think this is the most attention our Ben has ever directly given any object in his life and I can't help but believe that somehow this dog is responsible for that. This dog and my brother."

Now Sally had to stifle a sob. Hastily placing the urn back on its pedestal, she returned to her seat next to May.

"Thank you," the young minister said to Sally before addressing the other guests present. "Would anyone else like to share a memory or say a few words at this time? I'm sure that if Sam were here, he would love it if you did."

The guests all glanced nervously about, hoping someone would step up and find some words or anecdotes to impart but no one came forward. No one in the group had known him well enough to offer a reminiscence.

May's attention was directed toward her son as she watched his uncharacteristic fascination with the object of his grandfather's remains. While she sat mystified, the minister called out a final appeal for volunteers to speak and at that exact moment, she saw Kane, still in a reclining position, shift his weight onto his right side and slowly turn his head over his left shoulder to face her. A very distinct sensation washed over her as he directed his vision straight into her eyes. She was consumed by an unmistakable impression that the dog was speaking to her.

"Stand and say something," the look seemed to tell her.

The other-worldly look induced a chill through her body. It was the same mystical feeling the dog had elicited at the reservoir, but somehow it did not make her fearful. Somehow instead she felt blissful.

His eyes remained locked on her for several seconds before slowly turning his head forward again as the minister began his closing comments.

As the service was concluded and the assembled guests around her stood and began saying their goodbyes to one another, May remained seated. She could not take her eyes off the collie before her as she endeavored to grasp an unseen signal which seemed to be telling her that a miraculous creature had come into her son's life.

Her reverie was finally cut short as Sally called out her name. As she stood, Paul placed an arm around her shoulder and Sally approached Ben and kneeled next to him, placing her hand on his back as a signal that it was time to leave. The boy stood and joined his family who was accepting condolences from the guests. Though he remained by Sally's side, he did not take his eyes off Kane who remained in front of the urn.

May meanwhile attempted to concentrate on the people around her but she, too, found herself frequently glancing at the dog nearby. However, her attention was soon drawn toward a young man in his late twenties, dressed in a dark sweater and tie who stepped forward with a friendly smile, shaking first Paul's hand and then her own as he addressed them.

"Please allow me to extend my most heartfelt condolences," he said to them. "I'm Nick Stanley. Perhaps Sam told you about me?"

"You know, I'm afraid he didn't," Paul replied. "But we're very pleased to meet you and thank you for coming down to say goodbye to him."

"Aaah," Nick nodded. "That pretty much sounds like the Sam I knew, that he wouldn't have mentioned me. I was part of the team who worked with him on his last project for Prometheacorp. That is, until he shut down the project."

"My father wasn't in touch with us for several years before he died," May told him.

Nick frowned sympathetically. "Oh," he said. "I'm sorry. Well, I know he could be a bit ornery at times but . . . ."

"A bit," May agreed.

Paul's attention was directed toward another guest, but May and Nick continued their conversation.

"Well, despite that orneriness," he continued. "He was awfully darn good to me. See, he kind of took me under his wing and mentored me. I learned a lot, and I'm very grateful for all he did for me."

May was charmed by the stranger's likable personality and extended an invitation to join their family and friends for an after-service gathering at the McLaughlin home.

"Oh, I couldn't impose," he replied.

"It wouldn't be an imposition," Elizabeth assured him.

May had forgotten that her daughter was by her side but wasn't surprised at her eagerness to have the handsome young man join them.

Elizabeth blushed as she realized that her eagerness was a bit overdone and as if in apology, she offered her hand in greeting.

"I'm Elizabeth," she said. "I'm Sam's granddaughter. I mean, we'd love to talk to you. I didn't really know my grandfather so it would be great to talk to someone who could sort of fill in the blanks."

"We'll be honored to have you join us," said Sally who was standing nearby. "You can follow me. It's not very far."

Nick humbly accepted and thanked them for the invitation as another guest stepped in to take his place in the line of well-wishers.

Sally gave a wink to Elizabeth before taking Ben's hand and leading him over to the spot where Kane still lay before the urn. Kneeling beside the dog, she stroked his head.

"Kane," she said gently. "There's nothing more you can do for him now. He's far beyond your reach. I know you're going to miss him, but I also know that someday, someday you'll see him again and you'll both enjoy wonderful long walks together. Until that time my friend, I know he would wish for nothing more than to have you take responsibility for Ben here. He's a very extraordinary young man, and he's going to need all the help you can give him for as long as you can give it. Come on, boy. It's time to go home."

Sally managed to stand and Kane finally, unhurriedly, lifted his head and gazed one final time at all that remained of the god he had loved. Gradually he stood, and with head lowered, walked beside Sally and Ben as they headed toward the parked cars.

The family was silent as Paul drove the car away from Sam's gravesite toward the exit. May was buried in thought regarding Kane's actions and occasionally looked over her shoulder at the beautiful collie who sat between her two children in the back seat.

Elizabeth's arm was around the dog and May did a double-take as she realized that Ben was petting him. The stroking of fur with the palm of his hand was repetitious, perhaps not unlike the incessant tapping he would make with his fingers that seemed to have become less frequent since Kane's arrival at the McLaughlin home. However, the boy's movement was slower now, in contrast to the nervousness his fast finger tapping had represented, and his relaxed posture told her he was comforted by the dog's presence.

As their car proceeded past the guard station at the exit, Paul had to suddenly apply his breaks as the guard whom they had encountered on their entrance now stepped before them with his hand raised, blocking the exit.

Eliciting a no-nonsense demeanor of stern authority, he stepped around to Paul's window as May sighed sarcastically, "Oh help us."

The window on Paul's side of the car remained rolled up, and he didn't offer to roll it down until the guard tapped on it. With no hurry, Paul lowered the window.

"Can you lower my window too, Dad?" asked Elizabeth. "It's hot back here."

"Oh sure," her dad replied, complying with her request.

"Sir," began the guard, clearing his throat. "You may recall that I specifically advised you against allowing a dog to accompany you on the premises."

"Yes, I do remember that," Paul said. "But you see . . . ."

"And I believe the dog is still with you," the guard interrupted.

Paul turned to look at Kane in the back seat.

"Yes, I believe he is," Paul agreed.

"Paul," May interrupted, "Don't . . . ."

"I need hardly tell you, sir," the guard intoned, preparing to deliver a discourse on the inadvisability of dogs in cemeteries, "that as a responsible parent, the example you set for your young son in the back seat there is both irresponsible and disrespectful."

Before he could continue his lecture a loud horn was sounded by a driver on the entrance side of the guard station, and an impatient male driver yelled out, "Hey! I'm running late. Can I get directions?"

A line of cars had once again begun to form at the entrance. Quickly losing his military demeanor again, he held up a finger to Paul and instructed him, "Don't go way. Stay right there."

As Paul contemplated under what authority a guard at a memorial park could keep them under any kind of custody, May expressed her outrage at the fellow's swagger.

While the discussion was taking place in the front seat, Elizabeth was startled as Kane suddenly stepped over her lap and leaped out the window.

"Hey!" Elizabeth exclaimed, and her parents turned to see what had caused the commotion.

The family watched with amazement as Kane ran into the guard station and approached the guard, whose attention was directed toward the map he was marking to assist the impatient guest waiting in the entrance lane. Without hesitation, Kane swiftly lifted a hind leg and quickly urinated on the guard's leg. Preoccupied with his job, the guard was completely unaware that he had been "marked" by the dog.

May started to yell out at Kane but stopped herself and Elizabeth had to place her hand over her mouth to stifle a loud, audible gasp.

In a matter of seconds, Kane returned to the car, jumped through the open back seat window, stepped over Elizabeth's lap, and returned to his place between the two children.

Paul took no hesitation in stepping on the accelerator as he raced from the memorial park guard station and out to the main highway.

Although May felt some guilt in joining in, Paul and Elizabeth laughed raucously at the scene they had just witnessed. For the rest of the ride home, they imagined the look on the guard's face as he finally became aware of the dampness on his uniformed leg and saw the puddle of liquid by his foot. Their laughter suitably relieved them of the sense of gloom in which they had been immersed. Kane received hugs from Elizabeth and commendation from Paul as he sat, panting proudly.

"There's a reason the 'no dogs rule' exists, you know, and the guy was just doing his job," May said shaking her head, embarrassed she had been part of such a prank. Nevertheless, she was unable to resist laughing herself, and she couldn't remember how long it had been since they had all laughed together. Glancing back at Kane she noticed, for the second time today another uncharacteristic behavior from her son.

Ben was smiling broadly.

CHAPTER NINE

A handful of guests gathered at the McLaughlin home to sample the dishes of food and the generous amount of wine that had been laid out. The conversations were cheerful, tempered with the occasional interval of consoling words. May had to repeat often her explanation as to why her father had been out of touch with her family for such a long time, Sally acquainted everyone with stories of Sam's scientific genius while Paul steered his remarks as far as possible away from any mention of the state of his business.

With the adults so occupied, Ben found it easy to slip amongst them undetected and unrestricted in his access to the food. Grabbing a dish of pitted black olives he joined Kane who lay in a corner away from the others. Lying next to him, the boy stuck the end of each fingertip into the pitted holes of the olives until he was wearing a complete set on each hand. He offered a bite from one of his embellished fingers to Kane who politely refused. Unfazed, Ben set about sucking the juice that clung to each olive.

With a glass of zinfandel in his hand, Nick wandered through the groups of guests, nodding a "hello" as he passed but never stopping to engage in any discussion. As he passed Sally, she leaned to him confidentially.

"On the backyard swing," she said to him with a smile.

"Pardon me?" he responded.

"Elizabeth. That's who you're looking for, isn't it?" Sally answered.

"Oh!" he exclaimed. He tried to appear as if the idea hadn't occurred to him, but now that it had, it might indeed be a good idea.

"Yes. Sure. Thank you."

He smiled and nodded to Sally as he turned to find the doorway leading to the back of the house. Sally pointed the way, and he rather awkwardly smiled his thanks back at her as he walked out the door, grabbing an open bottle of white wine from a table on his way out.

Nick found Elizabeth seated comfortably on a white, wooden two-person back door porch swing suspended from the sturdy limb of an ancient oak. She was nursing a glass of white wine, lost in thought, as she gazed at the vineyards surrounding the house. Strolling over to her side, he greeted her with a friendly smile and a cordial hello.

"Oh! Hello," Elizabeth said with surprise as she withdrew from her trance.

"It looks very restful out here," he said and pointed to the swing. "Mind if I join you for a bit?"

"Sure," she said, nervously moving to one side of the seat to make room for him.

Nick seated himself next to her but, for what may have been only one minute but seemed to Elizabeth an eternity, he said nothing as he surveyed the scenery before him, smiling and sipping his wine.

"Very restful," he finally said, nodding toward the fields.

Elizabeth nodded, as she took a sip from her glass.

Noticing that her glass was nearly empty, he offered the bottle he held in his hand.

"May I fill your glass?" he asked.

"Oh, thank you," she said taking another swift drink before holding out her glass for a refill.

As Nick poured, she noticed the glass he held in his hand. "Wait," she said. "You're drinking red."

"Yeah," he replied as he finished pouring. "But you're carrying a bottle of white."

"Oh. Yeah," Nick responded, looking at the bottle label as if he had been unaware of its contents.

Elizabeth laughed playfully and pointed a finger at him reproachfully.

"How did you know I was drinking white?" she asked with a sprightly grin. "Have you been watching me?"

Nick feigned embarrassment and admitted, "Well, not really watching you exactly, but . . . ."

Elizabeth eyed him with a look of lighthearted suspicion and realizing that she saw through what he had thought was a clever opening line, he lowered his head sheepishly.

"Well, yeah. I guess you could say that," he laughed. "But not in a stalker sort of way."

Elizabeth laughed.

"Hey," he said. "I thought that was a pretty good way to introduce myself. Didn't you think so?"

"I've heard worse," she said with a slight shrug.

"So," he said, setting the bottle down by his feet. "Let's see what I know about you so far. You're studying to be a small animal vet, and you are in your first year at UC Davis."

"How did you know that?" she asked.

Without replying to her question, he continued. "You have an autistic younger brother to whom you are extremely devoted, and you hope to one day specialize in treatment for elderly dogs. Am I right?"

Elizabeth looked at him quizzically.

"I worked with your grandfather," Nick continued. "Remember?"

"I didn't even think he knew that much about my life," she remarked. "Did he talk much about me?"

Nick took a drink of his wine and mused for a moment. "M-m-m-m. Not a lot. He was more or less a mentor to me, so we talked a lot, but I can't say the subject of his family came up very often. When he closed down the lab and moved all his research to his home, we no longer stayed in contact. I've been pretty busy looking for another job."

The screen door on the back porch slammed shut, and Elizabeth and Nick turned in their seat to see her brother approach them with Kane close behind. Ben leaned into Elizabeth's lap displaying the olives stuck to the tips of his fingers.

"My goodness!" Elizabeth exclaimed, feigning shock. "What happened to your fingers?"

Ben smiled and removed an olive from his right index finger with his mouth.

"Believe it or not, this is progress," Elizabeth confided to Nick. "When he was younger he talked a lot. He use to ramble on and on about the silliest things but after I left home for school, he pretty much shut down. I think the dog is helping him."

Nick noticed the dog who was sitting in front of them. Kane seemed to be studying him and it somehow suddenly made Nick feel slightly uncomfortable.

"A collie," Nick remarked. "You don't see many of them these days. What do you call him?"

Elizabeth looked at Nick with surprise. "This is Kane," she answered and then watched Nick's face, expecting recognition of the name. After a moment, noting that the name meant nothing to him, she added, "My grandfather's dog. He must have talked about him."

"Oh, of course!" came the hasty reply. "Kane. Right. No, he talked about him. Sure."

The response was unconvincing and left Elizabeth wondering. How could he have known her grandfather as well as he claimed yet not have been familiar with the one thing Sally often told her that the old man had loved most?

Inside the house, Sally was listening patiently as a guest who had introduced himself as a friend of the family, having learned of Sally's experience as a veterinarian, continued a protracted explanation of the symptoms his beloved Shih Tzu was experiencing. At length, feeling her patience waning, Sally managed to interrupt him with the excuse that it was very difficult to offer an opinion without first examining the dog.

"I'll tell you what, though," she advised. "Why don't you call the office tomorrow morning and make an appointment with one of our veterinarians? I'm sure they'd be very happy to provide you with an evaluation and quote an estimate for their services. I myself am retired I'm afraid. Excuse me."

Quickly stepping away from the gentleman, she hastened to seek out May. Finding her sitting on the couch between a group of ladies who were extolling the virtues of the cheesecake they were enjoying, Sally caught her eye and motioned to her from across the room. Politely excusing herself, May set her dessert on the coffee table before her and stood, crossing the room to be with her aunt.

Taking her arm and looking around the room, Sally said confidentially, "I need to talk to you."

Scanning the room for a spot that would allow some privacy but not finding one, she motioned for May to follow her down the hall. Once inside a guest bedroom where numerous women's coats and purses lay scattered about the bed, Sally pulled May inside and closed the door behind them.

"I thought you should know," Sally told May, looking her in the eye. "A representative from Prometheacorp came by your father's house while I was finishing with the packing. He wanted access to your father's papers, but I wouldn't let him in. He claims there may be information pertaining to a project your father was working on for his company and he says that information is Prometheacorp property. I don't know the legality of all that, but I did tell him that he would need a judge's permission to go through my brother's property."

"Did the guy accept that?" asked May.

"Not exactly," Sally replied. "In fact, he started to get a bit hostile, which was the wrong tactic to take with me. I wound up running him off the property."

"Good for you!" May said.

"But listen," Sally continued, brushing aside coats and purses to make room on the bed to sit and pulling May down beside her. "I went by the house yesterday just to check on things, and I had the distinct impression that someone had been there. Someone besides me. There isn't a lot left to get rid of, but it was very clear that someone did a thorough search of the place."

"It had to be the guy from Prometheacorp," May speculated.

"Seemed pretty certain to me," Sally agreed. "But they didn't find what they were looking for, that I know. I'd done a pretty good inventory, and there couldn't have been anything of value."

"Did you call the police?" May asked.

Sally shook her head. "Nothing missing. I couldn't prove it was Prometheacorp. But here's the thing: Whatever Sam was working on for them was pretty important, and they must be looking for whatever's left of it. I think he must have destroyed it, but they probably think he left it with someone in the family. Now, Sam used to tell me that some of the goons at that company can be pretty ruthless. So just be aware. That's all I'm saying."

"Are you sure?" May questioned. "I mean, they're a big international company. Would they stoop so low as to . . . ."

Sally waved her off. "Don't be naïve, May. There may be a lot of money involved."

"Well," May responded with a shrug. "If I had it I'd give it to them, I guess."

"Maybe you wouldn't," Sally said ominously. "Maybe you *shouldn't.*"

CHAPTER TEN

Elizabeth led the way along the narrow path known as Cold Spring Trail which had been her favorite hiking spot since her first walk years ago. Walking right behind her, Ben was having little trouble keeping up, and Kane remained close beside the boy, cautious of the waters that babbled along the creek beside which they were traveling and particularly wary of the areas where the mountainside dropped away a bit too precipitously to his liking.

Not that the dog was fearful for his own safety. He had hiked with Sam along many a mountain pathway since he was a young pup and ordinarily he would have found the hike exhilarating but his concern for Ben's safety did not allow him the freedom to savor the beauty all around them.

Having traveled inward through a substantial forest of live oak, the trail soon returned back to the creek, and a profusion of alders thickly covered with green leaves fluttered in the breeze overhead. There Elizabeth paused, not out of any need to rest nor was there any need to wait for Ben to catch up to her. In fact, he and Kane had no trouble matching her pace. The trio was instead waiting for Nick, some distance behind, who was panting heavily in a laborious effort to gain on them.

While they waited, Elizabeth dug her hand into the small backpack Ben transported on his back and fished out a plastic bottle of water from which she took a drink, and then offered it to Ben. Before accepting it, he removed his pack, set it in front of him and withdrew from it a portable dog bowl into which he poured some of the bottled water which he placed before Kane.

Elizabeth smiled at the boy's thoughtfulness and reflected on the changes that had come over him in the few short weeks she had been home. Rubbing one of Kane's ears as he drank, she studied his face intently as she considered the dog's influence on Ben's behavior and the intelligence he seemed to possess.

"I've never known such a smart dog," Elizabeth remarked to Sally one day.

Normally her great-aunt responded with a witticism or two when Elizabeth touched upon the subject. "Well, what would you expect from a genius like your grandfather?" she would typically respond. "He would expect nothing less from his own dog."

The last time Elizabeth broached the subject, however, Sally's demeanor suddenly turned serious.

"It might not be a good idea to share your observations about Kane with anyone outside the family," Sally warned.

Responding to the puzzled look on Elizabeth's face, Sally tried to make light of her admonition. Suddenly turning her frown to a smile, she quickly added that because Kane was not neutered, he might have breeders from all over the world lining up to breed their dogs to him if word got out that he was some kind of genius.

Elizabeth marked that Sally's hasty attempt to turn her warning into a joke and the skittish laugh that followed was unconvincing as was her hurried attempt to change the subject. Now several days after the episode, Elizabeth remained troubled.

"I could use a swallow of some of that water," Nick gasped as he finally joined his hiking partners where they had paused on the mountain trail.

She laughed at his display of exaggerated exhaustion but chose not to tease him further about how badly out of shape he was. She had done that enough before he fell behind them again a third time. Instead, she tossed him a bottle of water which he caught and quickly guzzled.

Wiping the sweat from his brow with the back of his arm, he attempted to catch his breath.

"It's all uphill! You didn't tell me it was all uphill," he gasped.

"It isn't all uphill," Elizabeth said with a quick shake of her head. "Look, you said you wanted to do something I enjoyed doing but if you're not up to the task . . . ."

"No, no," he replied, raising his hand to stop her. "My masculine pride has been impugned. Now I'm on a mission to restore my dignity. That is, after I catch my breath."

"OK," she said, pointing down a path. "Just a few steps in that direction is a great place to take a rest. That is if you're up to it."

"Lead on," he said, assuming a hearty pose.

Elizabeth took the empty bottle from him and tossed it into the backpack along with the water bowl and then assisted Ben as he slid back into the pack before leading the group toward the nearby rest stop. As she walked, she considered the personality of this guy she had been dating for the last few weeks since her grandfather's funeral. Never mind that he was a few years older, he was fun, great personality, good sense of humor, relatively intelligent, sensitive and, oh yes, good looking. There had to be a defect somewhere so she figured that being physically unfit must be it.

After a trek of only a few minutes, the hikers halted before a small clearing that opened on a beautiful twin-spouted waterfall. Overlooking the picturesque pool before them sat a quaint wooden bench upon which Nick quickly collapsed with a groan.

"Pardon my lack of chivalry," Nick panted. "This is an emergency."

"No special treatment expected," Elizabeth replied as she sat next to him.

Ben walked to the side of the pool, dumped his backpack and fell to his knees, sticking a hand into the cool water. Joining him, Kane sniffed the pool cautiously.

"You probably shouldn't drink that water, Kane," Elizabeth called out to him.

The dog immediately lifted his head and looked in her direction before returning his attention to Ben.

Kane's reaction caught Nick's attention. "He looked just like he understood what you said," he noted.

"He probably did," Elizabeth said with a nod.

Ben picked up a stick and poked it in the water as he and Kane walked along the water's edge, distancing themselves from Elizabeth and Nick, but still within view. Occasionally the boy would pick up a rock, examine it and then toss it into the stream.

"How much vocabulary do dogs possess?" Nick wondered.

"The average dog, about a hundred sixty-five words," she answered with a shrug. "They can be taught more. The record is over a thousand."

Nick shook his head. "That's more than a lot of humans I know if you don't count profanity."

Still trying to make sense of Sally's warning regarding Kane's intelligence, she opted to change the subject.

"I meant to ask," she said. "How's the job hunting coming along?"

"I got a friend sending me a few jobs I can work on from home," he replied. "Web designs and stuff. Should pay enough to allow me to survive on bread and water for a few more months until a real job turns up."

"Well, we expect you at our house tonight for a real dinner. You're coming, right?"

"I've been sponging off your mom's generosity pretty regularly. Tomorrow night it's my turn. I'll take you to dinner for a change. The Squat and Gobble. Great food."

"I've heard of that place."

"Anything you want from their menu, as long as it's hamburger."

Kane and Ben had paused in their stroll along the creek to examine a collection of stones. Ben sat on a boulder and closely examined several of them while Kane pawed through a small pile of pebbles, searching for one that might interest the boy. Coming across one that contained an interesting pattern of white markings, Kane dunked his muzzle into the water and fished it out with his mouth, clutching it with his teeth. Turning to Ben, he dropped it in his lap and sat waiting for his response.

Ben looked down from the rock he had been studying, then tossed it aside before picking up the stone Kane had delivered. The dog watched him intently as he rolled the object around in his hand, inspecting its design, feeling its texture as he rubbed it with his thumb. After repeating these actions for a minute or two, he held the stone in front of Kane's face, as if expecting a comment or reaction from him but the dog looked past the stone into Ben's face.

Not getting the reaction he had expected, Ben continued to thrust the stone before the dog. When at last he realized no reaction was forthcoming, Ben stood and thrust the hand with the stone angrily toward Kane's face and finally shouted, "See? See?"

Kane barked excitedly.

From her position down the creek, Elizabeth stopped her conversation with Nick in mid-sentence when she heard Ben's voice. Suddenly standing, she looked in disbelief as Kane ran circles around Ben, who laughed as he held forth the stone in his hand.

With a gasp, she rushed to Ben's side, Nick close behind her. Reaching him, she laughed with excitement as Ben held the rock high for her to see and continued shouting, "See? See?"

Elizabeth grabbed his wrist and replied, "Yes! I see! I see!" Glancing at Nick, she asked, "Did you hear that?"

"Yeah," Nick said with some uncertainty.

Elizabeth shouted with excitement, "He's talking! He hasn't done anything like that for years, and he's not just repeating what he hears. Ben's talking! That's great!"

She stood and grabbed the boy, lifting him off his feet and spinning him around as Ben continued to repeat, "See? See?"

"Yes," she exclaimed. "I see! I see, my boy!"

"That's really great," Nick said in an attempt to join in Elizabeth's jubilation.

At their feet, Kane shared the excitement, barking loudly.

With Elizabeth twirling her brother around and bouncing up and down with him she was far too animated for Nick to attempt any sort of congratulatory hug. Instead, he opted to share the moment with Kane reaching for him and quickly roughing the fur behind his neck.

Kane retreated from Nick's touch, his mood suddenly shifting from playful to disapproval with alarming speed. The dog backed away from him, his ears flat upon his head, his tail tucked tightly between his legs, the rough around the nape of his neck noticeably erect, and it was gravely clear that Nick's gesture was unquestionably unwelcome. Nick felt a sudden jolt of fear at the lightning speed with which Kane's temperament changed.

His head held low, not taking his eyes off Nick, the dog slowly moved to place Elizabeth and Ben between them. His expression could only be interpreted as one of displeasure.

Elizabeth and Ben were still too wrapped up in their celebration to notice the sudden exchange that had taken place right beside them as they laughed and played together.

For his part, Nick doubted he would ever again attempt to befriend Kane.

CHAPTER ELEVEN

Over the next few days and weeks, Ben continued to open up. As if tasked with an urgent need to make up for the large gap in his young years in which he had stopped speaking, he would often go through spells in which words flew rapidly from his mouth in a seemingly unending stream. Though the subject of his ceaseless chatter would frequently change, sometimes in mid-sentence, his eagerness to share all of the limitless thoughts that overflowed from his brain compelled him to speak with dizzying speed.

While May was astonished at the change that had come over her son she would occasionally beg him to slow down, to gather his thoughts, and she pleaded with him to try to stick to one subject at a time, but her entreaties went unheeded. Ben was again outgoing as he had once been but when he was blabbering, he was uninterested in or incapable of accepting any thoughts or words from anyone else. It required considerable effort to calm his ramblings.

For his part, Kane was at turns amused and indifferent, but generally, this change in his boy seemed unimportant, and he was willing to accept him without judgment regardless of Ben's disposition. As long as Ben was not upset or displeased, Kane was content.

May never ceased to be amazed at the dog's capacity for acceptance, and she would often find herself talking to him as if he were human and capable of understanding every word she spoke. In time she came to believe that he did.

During visits, Sally observed Kane closely and was often seen nodding her approval as May related innumerable stories of the dog's behavior and of his interaction with Ben.

"It's as if Ben and Kane understand each other's thoughts," May said to her one day.

Standing next to her as they watched the boy and dog interact, Sally placed an arm around May's shoulder and gave her a hug.

On one of several occasions on which Nick was expected for dinner, May returned home after an expedition to the grocery store and found him sitting on the front porch engrossed in the cellular phone he held in his hand. Ben and Kane unloaded themselves from the backseat of the car and passed Nick on their way to the front door of the house. Nick called out a friendly greeting to Ben, but the boy and his dog continued past without acknowledging him.

Nick was not expected for at least another hour, and May expressed her surprise at his early arrival.

"Yeah, I know," Nick responded. "I finished my work early so I thought I may as well pop over and see if there was anything I could do to help you out."

"Well, you can help me haul in the groceries for starters," May said, opening the car trunk. "Elizabeth won't be home from the clinic for a bit."

"Yeah, I called her," Nick said as May handed him two sizable sacks of groceries. "She said to come on over. Hope that's okay."

"Of course it's okay," she confirmed, grabbing a third sack from the trunk of the car.

As she started to close the trunk lid, Nick stopped her.

"What's that?" Nick said pointing to an item that had been pushed to the back of the trunk. "Do you need to take that in?"

May grimaced as she noticed the box her father had left for her.

"Oh, I guess I might as well," she said with a sigh. "It's been back there long enough."

She awkwardly placed the box under her free arm over which she had slung her purse while simultaneously continuing to close the trunk. Noticing Nick's curious look, she explained. "Something my father left me. I have no idea what it is."

"Supposed to be something very important according to Sally," May said sarcastically as she held the front door open so Nick could pass through.

"You sound doubtful," Nick said. "You've never opened it?"

May managed to place the box between the Tiffany lamp and the telephone which sat upon a round table in the corner of the front room as she balanced the bag of groceries in her other arm.

"I left the key in my purse, I think," she said over her shoulder as she hung the straps of her purse over the handle of the doorway leading to the kitchen as she passed through. "It can wait. Maybe after dinner tonight."

Nick remained in the front room, his eyes on the box. After a moment, May's voice called him from the kitchen. "What's holding you up? Kitchen's in here." He pulled himself away and joined her.

Though she was unable to pinpoint the source, Elizabeth sensed that everyone at dinner that evening was somehow distracted. She had arrived home from the clinic not soon after Nick and her mother had unpacked the groceries.

Pulling a bottle of beer from the refrigerator and handing it to Nick, she chattered away about her day and the animals she and her great aunt had treated, but he didn't seem to hear her and only occasionally offered a nod or a verbal acknowledgment. His mind was elsewhere.

Elizabeth looked toward her mother who was busying herself with dinner preparations, but she was too preoccupied with that activity to notice. Finally, Elizabeth stopped talking to see if anyone would notice but no one did. With a sigh of exasperation, she announced that she was going to change out of her veterinary scrubs before dinner.

Pausing by the doorway, she glanced back at Nick and her mother. He had set down his beer and was setting dishes on the table while her mother searched for an ingredient in a cupboard. Elizabeth rolled her eyes and departed unnoticed.

Finding Ben was seated on the bottom step of the stairway leading to the upper part of the house playing with a small toy car, she sat beside him.

Reaching over to Kane, who lay nearby, she stroked his head as he looked up into her face.

"How's that for irony?" she addressed the dog. "You're the only one in the house that will listen to me."

Kane brought himself into a sitting position with a look that invited her to pour her heart out.

Scratching his neck, she asked, "What goes on in that incredible mind of yours? What is it you're not telling us?"

Kane leaned his head into her as he enjoyed the pleasure of Elizabeth's touch. His eyes closed in contentment, and for a while she remained with him, both of them deriving a sense of relaxation from each other.

By the time Elizabeth leisurely made her way up to her room and changed her clothes and returned to the dining room, her father had returned home from an appointment he had been attending in town. He didn't seem to notice her as she took her seat next to Nick at the table.

At first, Elizabeth attempted to carry the bulk of the conversation throughout the meal, but she was the only one with anything to contribute. She even invited Ben to join in but was warned off by May who cautioned that once ignited, his talk might be difficult to subdue. Instead, his mother told him not to forget to eat his green beans.

At the end of the meal, Elizabeth set down her fork. "Well what's going on around here?" she asked. "Would anyone care to tell me what this cloud is that's hanging over this table tonight?"

May looked up from her plate toward Paul who glanced back at her. Finally, he stopped eating long enough to speak.

"We need to have a family talk," he said with hesitation. "Sorry, Nick."

Nick pushed his chair back from the table. "No. No. That's okay. I'll just . . . ."

"Why don't we go into the den," May interrupted, rising from her chair.

"Sure," Nick said apologetically. "I'll call you later, Elizabeth."

Elizabeth motioned him back down. "No. Wait here," she said. "We probably won't be long, will we Dad?"

Paul assured her with a shake of his head that they would not.

"Okay," Nick offered eagerly, looking around the table. "You guys go ahead, and I'll clear all this up."

"Thank you," May said with a smile. "Make yourself a cup of coffee."

"I'll put on a pot," he replied, starting to gather dishes from the table.

Paul offered a half smile as he led the way to the den, followed by his family. With Ben and Kane following, the door was closed behind them.

As Elizabeth sat on the bench before the piano that dominated the room, May sat on the love seat, and Paul plopped down in a large armchair, markedly uncomfortable. Ben sat on the floor at his mother's feet and was inspecting a toy airplane he had forgotten beneath the bench while Kane was nearby sitting sharply at attention.

Paul's furrowed expression as he surveyed the room cast a pall over the meeting and compelled Elizabeth to dread words that had not yet even been spoken. May's expression implied that Paul had already shared the news with her.

"I'm going to be going away for a while," Paul started.

Though he did not look up, Ben stopped fidgeting with the toy he held in his hands.

Before Elizabeth could ask, her father continued. "Afghanistan."

Elizabeth's chin dropped.

"I'll be working in construction for a company called Strendicorp," Paul said. The money I'll make will help us get back on our feet and save this place. I'll be gone a year, and I'm assured that I'll be working in a safe, secure location."

May turned her head and stared out the window, but she really wasn't looking at anything.

"Dad!" Elizabeth nearly yelled. "It's a war zone! There is no place safe over there. That's why it's called a war zone. You can't do this!"

"I'll be all right," he said in what he hoped was a comforting tone.

Elizabeth rushed to him and threw herself down before him, grabbing his knees.

"Don't! Don't go!" she pleaded nearly sobbing. "You'll be gone a year. What if you never come back?"

May called out to her. "Elizabeth . . . ."

"It'll be fine, sweetheart," Paul said, placing his hands on Elizabeth's shoulders.

As he spoke those words, the adults in the room became aware of a sound that started out softly like a long, hushed moan, gradually rising in intensity until it resembled the blare of a police siren.

Ben was still sitting near the piano bench, the fingers of his hand hanging from his open mouth as he woefully wailed an anguished cry.

May reached him first, promptly followed by Elizabeth. Together they attempted to console him.

"He must have understood what Dad was saying," Elizabeth said to her mother. "Sometimes he understands everything we say. You can never be sure."

Paul ran his fingers through his hair with a frustrated gesture, but he made no attempt to comfort his son whose howl was now lessening to a sob.

Pushing his mother and sister angrily aside, Ben rushed to Kane who was standing close by. He fell on his knees and buried his face in the collie's soft, white rough which stifled his sobs.

With Ben clinging to his neck, Kane looked up into Paul's red-rimmed eyes with a reproachful look that was unmistakable. The look in the dog's eyes generated a sudden, heavy sense of guilt and shame in Paul unlike any he had ever borne before as tears of remorse blurred his vision.

May tried to rub Ben's back in a gesture that often helped soothe him in times past, but he persistently pushed her hand away, his head still buried amid Kane's fur. Resigning herself to her inability to comfort her son, she suggested to Kane that he accompany him upstairs to his room until he felt better.

Turning toward the door, Ben still clinging tightly, Kane moved to obey her wish. May opened the door to allow the two of them to pass before closing it behind them and returning to her place on the love seat.

The three of them sat in silence for a minute or two, Paul struck with the unspoken words of reproof he had received from Kane. Elizabeth still sat on the floor where she had tried to comfort Ben as she stared before her with a look of disbelief over her father's decision while May once again looked blankly in the direction of the window.

Gradually Paul found words to speak.

"It's really the best solution," he assured them. "I'll be leaving in a few weeks and until then we'll . . . ."

Suddenly there came from the next room the sound of angry barking. Elizabeth and May had never heard Kane bark that way with such urgency and fury, and it took them a moment to fully comprehend what they were hearing before they could respond. While Paul remained seated, the two women rose to their feet and raced out the door through which Kane and Ben had just passed.

Rushing through the dining room they were in too much hurry to notice that the table had not been cleared. In the front room, they saw the screen door closing as if someone had just passed through. With Kane's barking coming from outside the house they rushed to the door, pulled it open and hastened through to the front porch.

Elizabeth and May stopped short at the front steps, bewildered at the action taking place before them. As he continued to bark, Kane had chased Nick to his car. The car door was slammed in the dog's face as Nick immediately started the engine, shifted into gear and accelerated with such panic and speed that dirt and gravel shot out from the rear wheels, raising a dust storm as he steered the car out through the front gate. Nick didn't even pause as he turned out of the driveway on to the main highway, the car nearly flipping over in the process due to the careless speed he took the turn, his tires screeching as he rushed away. Kane followed closely behind the vehicle and stopped only at the highway, still barking as he watched Nick disappear from sight.

"Kane!" Elizabeth shouted at him. "Stop that! What got into you? Come here! Come!"

The dog stopped barking but watched until he was certain Nick was long gone. Once assured, he turned and trotted back to Elizabeth and May.

"I've never seen him act like that," May said with astonishment. "Poor Nick! He must have been terrified."

Elizabeth studied the dog who now sat before her. He was not cowed but returned her look with an expression of satisfaction.

"He's never warmed up to Nick for some reason," Elizabeth said. "I wonder what in the heck . . . . I'd better call him."

As she opened the door, Kane rushed ahead of them and once inside they saw him seated next to Ben who sat silently at the foot of the stairs.

Paul soon joined them, asking as to the cause of the commotion and May explained as Elizabeth picked up the phone and dialed Nick's cell phone number.

After several rings, she pushed the disconnect button on the phone and dialed again before remarking, "He's not answering. Must be scared out of his wits."

As she stood waiting for an answer to her call, she idly touched the lid of the box that May had sat near the phone earlier that evening.

"What's this?" she asked.

Glancing up from Ben momentarily, May replied, "A box my dad left me."

"What's in it?" Paul asked.

"Oh, I don't know," she replied. "I haven't opened it yet."

Looking back up at the box May stopped short. With the phone still to her ear, Elizabeth had opened the lid and was sifting through the contents of the box.

"How sweet of him," Elizabeth remarked. "There's a lot of old pictures and family mementos in here. He must have thought these were things you'd enjoy keeping."

Confused, May looked toward her purse where the key to the box had been deposited, but now she noticed that one of the two straps on the bag hung loose on the door handle. Had she left it hanging that way without realizing it? Looking back at the open lid of the box she knew she had not. The key was in the lock.

Elizabeth hung up the telephone.

"Maybe I should drive to his place and check on him," she said.

"I don't think you should, sweetheart, May replied, looking back at Kane. She knew exactly why he had chased Nick away.

CHAPTER TWELVE

The main headquarters of Prometheacorp resided within a two-story building situated in a campus-like setting surrounded by large rolling mountains and a thickly wooded area. Though the Northern California location was not zoned for business or for any structures at all for that matter, the right amount of money in the right pockets paid for the persuasion and permits required, streamlining the whole approval process. Chief Executive Officer Tom Burch convinced his fellow officers that locating business operations in an area considered remote by most industry standards would better enable him to control his organization and allow his extensive security staff greater power to control trade secrets from competitors. The Prometheacorp Public Relations Department put a different spin on it: the headquarters, surrounded by 25-foot high chain link fences heavily patrolled by armed security and guard dogs was a tranquil setting designed to relax their loyal employees and free their minds to innovate, invent and pioneer new technologies and products.

On the other hand, computers, as Burch was constantly reminded, were much harder to control regardless of how much armed security and specially trained guard dogs were on the payroll. It was a matter of no little annoyance to him and the reason for the existence of an extensively staffed department whose only function was to prevent unauthorized access to files and to plug leaks. Unfortunately, the Cyber Security Department became so thorough in its duty that other departments within the organization were often restricted from performing their jobs effectively, which constituted an additional source of irritation for the company CEO.

Burch was quite used to buying whatever was needed to complete a company project, so when members of his creative staff began work on a special top-secret program but were unable to successfully complete it with the personnel and resources currently employed, a talent search was undertaken. An extensive global hunt yielded one name above all others who possessed the unrivaled qualities most likely to produce the needed result.

The man's name was Sam Crisp.

To Burch's great displeasure, however, after presenting Sam a generous offer of employment following a brief visit to the Prometheacorp headquarters, the prospective employee announced that under no circumstances and regardless of the amount of money offered would he work within the organization's carefully maintained base of operations. It had taken Sam only a cursory review of the company's working conditions for him to surmise that he would be unable to successfully complete his task in what he referred to as a stockade. He would agree to design and complete the project only at a location to be chosen by him near his home in Lynmoore.

With great indignation, Burch begrudgingly ordered Sam to cool his heels while he consulted his associates as to the acceptability of the counter-offer. During a private conference, Burch and his aides struck upon what they felt was an acceptable compromise. Sam would be allowed to pursue the project at his location with no interference from upper management provided that all personnel working under him would be subject to selection and approval by Burch himself. It was further understood that no work was to be performed outside the chosen facility and that every detail of the work performed there would remain absolutely top secret and that every bit of data, every computer and every scrap of paper would be retained and would be the sole property of Prometheacorp. *Absolutely* (the word was circled on the contract in pen by Tom Burch, and Sam was required to initial it).

Burch and his staff figured that with their own personnel choices working on the project they could plant enough reliable spies in place to ensure Sam's compliance with their terms and thereby maintain control. It was not what Burch would have liked, but the potential for profit that the project promised was too great an opportunity to be lost over such details.

Now that Sam was dead, Burch refused to believe that the project data no longer existed despite the old man's denial to the contrary. The workers on the program all testified that as soon as they had gotten close to producing results, Sam suddenly became uncommunicative and all believed he continued working on it in secret. Burch reasoned that when Sam knew he was certain to die soon, he wouldn't have continued to develop the project if he hadn't intended to pass on the secret to someone. Who else would that have been if not his own family?

That's where Nick Stanley came in. He was an eager up and coming young engineer in Burch's employ, and when he was briefed on the significance of the project, he pledged to the executives in charge to do whatever his company might require of him in order to locate the data needed to produce it.

"Short of murder," he said, chuckling. The executives didn't laugh.

Now Nick was seated behind a conference table in a room adjacent to Burch's office filling in Dawn Elder, Burch's zealous second-in-command, on his observations and accomplishments during his surveillance of the McPherson family. Ms. Elder had just finished her interview, concluding that the entire undercover operation was a washout when Burch eagerly busted through the door accompanied by a thin, bearded and bespectacled older man with a professorial demeanor.

"Now," Burch said, seating himself at the head of the table, dramatically folding his hands and leaning in to Nick. "What do we have?"

Nick didn't want to be the one to break the bad news to the CEO, but he was saved from that task by Elder.

"Nothing," she said.

Burch stared at Nick for what seemed like a very long time before repeating, "Nothing."

Nick wasn't sure what he could add to that announcement, but his boss continued staring at him as if expecting him to elaborate. "Nothing?" Burch repeated.

Compelled to break Burch's piercing stare, he finally replied, "Well, I thought I was on to something. There was a box the old man left Missus McLaughlin. She'd been told he left her something very important but, well, when I had a chance to break it open it only had a bunch of personal family pictures and stuff like that."

Burch didn't break his position. "Uh huh," he said.

Nick nodded, but Burch seemed to want him to say more, and he could feel droplets of sweat starting to roll down his forehead.

"No project data or formulas or anything like that," Nick finally managed to say.

Finally, Burch turned to his executive assistant and asked, "He's going back?"

"Well actually," Nick stammered, "that would be difficult. I was caught breaking into the box and had to leave quickly so, no, it won't be possible for me to go back."

Burch was staring down at his hands which were still clasped and resting on the table before him. A slight frown wrinkled his brow.

"See, I was not sure when I'd have the opportunity to get into the box again," Nick started, "so I had to take a chance, but . . . ."

"Do you mean to tell me," Burch suddenly interrupted, looking Nick straight in the eye again, "that he didn't leave anything else to his own family?"

"Nothing I could find," Nick said with a shrug. "Nothing except the box and, um, a dog. A very smart dog."

Now Burch stared at him in disbelief. After another prolonged pause, he finally reclined back in his seat, looking toward the ceiling and clasping his hands on his forehead, moaning in disbelief. Eventually, he stood and stretched his back, staring out the large window that dominated the room. Shaking his head, he turned to leave but was stopped before he could reach the door.

Kenneth Matheson, the bearded professor, had remained standing throughout the interchange as if deep in thought but now, as Burch started to pass him on the way out, he held up a hand to stop him as if struck by a sudden realization.

"Hold on!" he said. The senior executive stopped and waited while his associate continued his thought.

Approaching Nick, he asked suspiciously, "A very smart dog?"

"A *very* smart dog," Nick confirmed, turning to Elder.

"How smart?" Matheson asked.

Nick thought it over before responding, "He seems pretty darn smart. A collie dog." Turning to Elder, he asked, "They're supposed to be pretty smart, aren't they? Collies? Lassie and all that stuff?"

"That's it," she said, looking back at the professor.

Burch thought it over a moment. "Maybe," he said.

Elder stood and approached her boss. "Let me take Kenneth here, and someone from legal," she said. "I want to meet this dog."

"His name is Kane," Nick offered.

Burch was becoming excited. "Don't offer them any money. Not yet. Tell them that legally the dog belongs to Prometheacorp. See if they'll listen to reason. We won't apply any pressure at first."

"Not until we have to," Elder interjected.

"He left the dog to Ben, his grandson," Nick said, though deep inside he knew it made no difference to Burch. "The boy is autistic. The dog helps him."

The other three in the room had already tuned him out. They were talking enthusiastically among themselves as they hurried from the room, leaving Nick alone at the table, awash in dread and remorse.

"Please leave him be," Nick said feebly to no one there.

CHAPTER THIRTEEN

Ben's ability to participate in a back and forth conversation and to interact with others was accelerating. Inevitably he would manage to steer the topic of any conversation back to his dog, but everyone was so pleased with the boy's rapid progress no one was inclined to complain. Though the casual visitor couldn't help but notice some peculiarities in Ben's speech patterns, his habit of repeating some questions asked of him or his sometimes uncommon responses, patience would eventually yield an acknowledgment, comprehension, and relevant reply. An exceptional degree of intelligence beyond his age began to emerge, confirming a suspicion May had held for many years.

On the front step of the house each morning, Ben methodically brushed Kane with a wire dog brush, patiently removing enormous clusters of fur which he would pull from the bristles of the grooming tool and place in a large paper shopping bag. The other members of his family were grateful that Ben was diligent about the dog brushing chore because to all of them it seemed that since Kane started shedding his winter coat in anticipation of the warm summer months to come there was no end to the prodigious quantity of fur the collie managed to produce. May and Elizabeth were certain that for every fiber pulled from his skin at least two dozen sprouted to take its place. Ben didn't mind the task however and in fact, found it therapeutic. Kane found it blissful.

As Nick very slowly pulled his car up in front of the McLaughlin home, he found Ben performing his daily routine with Kane and the dog brush. Turning off the ignition, he watched for a moment before looking carefully around to see if anyone else was nearby and after satisfying himself that they were alone he gently opened the car door and cautiously stepped out, pausing to gauge Kane's reaction.

Ben languidly continued to brush while Kane remained still, carefully watching the visitor.

Lifting both of his hands over his head, Nick addressed the dog directly in a quiet, delicate voice.

"Kane," he began, "I know you have reason to mistrust me. I appreciate that. I have earned your mistrust. But I need to talk to Ben. I have something extremely important to say to him . . . to say to both of you."

Kane continued to stare at him without blinking.

"Extremely important. *Extremely* important," Ben replied.

Kane looked at the boy and then back at Nick.

"Ben," he called out, trying to seize his attention.

The boy looked up at him.

"You don't have to be afraid of Kane. He won't hurt you," Ben said.

Tentatively lowering his hands Nick took a few cautious steps toward them.

"Unless he has to," Ben added, resuming his brushing activity.

Nick stopped suddenly, but after carefully pondering Kane's unbroken stare he managed to muster a bit of bravery which until now had been unfamiliar to him. Somehow the collie conveyed to him an expression that seemed to say, "I don't trust you, but you are not in danger. For now."

Pointing to a spot on the step next to Ben, Nick asked, "May I sit?"

Ben began singing a verse from "I Am the Walrus," about sitting in an English garden waiting for the sun.

Uncertain whether that signified permission, Nick hesitated a moment before sitting. Not totally comfortable talking to a young autistic boy and his dog, he struggled, searching for a way to begin.

"Ben," he started tenuously, "and . . . and Kane, I came here expecting to talk to your mother but since what I have to say really pertains directly to the two of you and since you'll be the one who will soon have to make a very big decision, maybe it's best I have this conversation with the two of you."

"Something important?" Ben asked, halting in mid brush stroke.

"Yeah," Nick confirmed, "pretty important. See . . . . Well, first of all, your grandfather, see, he, well, to sort of simplify it, he invented this computer chip, see, and this computer chip makes people smarter. He put this computer chip inside of Kane. Somewhere back here …"

Nick started to indicate the area by touching Kane's head, but the dog suddenly jerked away. Nick quickly withdrew his hand.

"Well," he continued, "I'm not certain where he put the microchip, but it's somehow connected to the frontal and temporal lobes of his brain, and it makes him very smart."

"Why did Grandpa do that?" Ben asked. "Kane is already smart." Ben began reciting a long list of things Kane had done recently, but Nick interrupted.

"I'm sure that's true," Nick agreed, "but this microchip makes him even smarter. Smarter than all other dogs and probably a lot of humans. But, see, this company that your grandfather worked for paid him to make this microchip, so they own it. They're gonna want it back."

"Well," said Ben resuming his brushing, "If they own it they can have it. Kane doesn't need it."

"Yeah, that's where it gets complicated," Nick responded. "Since the computer chip is inside Kane this company needs to see how your grandfather was able to make it work. The computer chip by itself isn't any use to them if they can't take everything apart and see how it's connected. They need to know that so they can make more of the computer chips and put them inside people to make them smarter."

"How are they going to take it apart if it's inside Kane?" Ben asked.

"Oh boy," Nick declared, rising and pacing. He was trying to figure a delicate way to break it to him.

But Ben figured it out for himself.

"They wouldn't be able to do that unless . . . ." The realization was dawning on him. ". . . Unless they take Kane apart."

Nick stopped his pacing and faced the boy. "Yeah," he said, relieved that at least that part of his disclosure was out. "They're gonna want to do a lot of medical experiments on him. Maybe take him apart and hook him up to machines and stuff. I'm not so sure if that would be a good thing. I thought maybe you could help me figure this out."

Ben threw down his brush. "Why? Why do they want that thing?" he asked.

"Well . . . , " Nick said with hesitation, "that microchip is worth a lot of money. A lot of money. The company could charge people maybe millions of dollars to get one of these things."

"Everybody? Then everybody would be smart," Ben concluded.

Nick shook his head. "No, not everybody, I'm afraid. That would be a good thing, wouldn't it? If poor people could get hooked up to one of those microchips, it could help make them smarter and get opportunities to do things they might not otherwise get to do."

"Opportunities." Ben contemplated the word.

"Yeah," Nick explained. "Chances. More chances for a better life."

"So if they take Kane apart," Ben mused, "they'll give this thing to the poor people?"

"I don't think so. Only rich people."

Ben stomped his foot in anger. "That's not right!"

Nick was proud of the boy. "So, what do you think you'll do if they come here and want to give you lots of money for Kane?"

"I'll tell Kane to bite 'em in the ass!" Now Ben was running around Kane, hitting the air with his hands.

Though apprehensive that this small boy could fend off an immense corporation with attorneys, with millions to buy off anyone in the way, and with a CEO like Tom Burch in charge, Nick nevertheless smiled, considering the possibility. His purpose in driving to the McLaughlin home had been achieved, and he figured it best to get back to work before his employers noticed his absence or in case Elizabeth should return home from work. He wasn't prepared to face her wrath, justified though it might be.

The thought of Elizabeth reminded him of another purpose for making the trip. Reaching into his jacket breast pocket, he withdrew an envelope. It had been torn open, and the name "May" was written across the front followed by the words, "To be opened only after my death."

Nick weighed the envelope in his hand before reaching again into his breast pocket and pulling out a pen. He quickly wrote a message on the back of the envelope, stopping once to consider his words before resuming his notation and signing his name.

Ben was still actively boxing the air as Nick called his name in an effort to get his attention.

"Listen," Nick said. "I have a mission for you . . . ."

"A mission!" Ben shouted, imitating a jet airplane and continuing his run around Kane. "Bite 'em in the ass, Kane!"

"Yeah," Nick said. Managing to grab the boy's arm, he firmly placed the envelope in his hand, closing Ben's fingers over it.

"Give this envelope to your mother right away, Ben," the boy was commanded. "Can you remember to do that?"

Looking at the dog, Nick asked, "Can you make sure he does that, Kane?"

Kane looked at the envelope before replying with a reassuring bark.

"Good. Thank you," Nick said and then mused to himself as he turned and walked to his car, "I'm talking to a dog."

As Nick turned his car up the driveway to return to the highway, he glanced into his side view mirror long enough to see Ben and Kane enter the house. He blushed as he thought of the theft he had committed against the wonderful family that had befriended him and the betrayal for which he was responsible. Accelerating his vehicle down the road, the embarrassment was replaced by worry over the boy, the dog, and the lengths to which Prometheacorp would go to separate them and to possess Kane and the secret that resided within him.

CHAPTER FOURTEEN

Dear May

If Sally has carried out my wishes, I expect that when you read this letter, I will already be dead. I'm sorry if that's just a little abrupt, but you probably remember how much I always hated euphemisms. I didn't "pass away." I'm dead.

That's not the way I wanted to begin this letter, so maybe I better start over. I've been taking medications that sometimes make it a little tough to think straight, so I admit I sometimes tend to rattle on. This is a letter of apology, but that's not what I want to apologize for.

What I really want to apologize about is for not being there for you these many years. I don't know if you'll believe me, but it has been so very hard for me to stay away and when I think how much I've missed by not being a part of your life and when I consider how much love and laughter I could have shared with you and the children my heart is just torn apart.

This is kind of tough explaining to you why I've stayed out of touch, and I don't know if you'll believe me when I explain it to you but just consider this: you know I don't believe in an afterlife, so I have no reason to lie to you. I'm not around in some ghostly form or sitting on a cloud up in the sky with wings on looking down at you, but I think it's time for you to know the truth.

From the day you brought Paul home to meet your mom and me I didn't trust him. I can't say why but it wasn't just that no man was good enough for my only daughter. I just always had a feeling that he was more caught up in himself than he was in you and after Elizabeth was born, I could plainly see that he hadn't really wanted to be a father. I think he probably grew to be proud of her, but I've always wondered how he dealt with Ben and his special needs. I'd always pretend not to be listening to Sally all the times she'd be telling me about what's been going on with your family. I guess I was never comfortable with anybody seeing my pain, but the truth is I relished every bit of news she shared with me.

Although I never really liked Paul, I nonetheless wanted you to be happy. Whenever he and I got together we always somehow managed to get into an argument. I don't know if you remember it that way, but Paul always seemed to start it. It always seemed to me that he was jealous of the bond you and I had and it was a real irritation to him that I was closer to you than he could ever be. I guess some guys are just like that and it irked him just to have me around.

One day I guess he just had enough. You weren't there when it happened but he latched on to some excuse or other to cuss me out down one side and up another, and I finally broke. I punched him a good one on the jaw, and he went down hard. It's a good thing he had enough sense not to come back at me because I don't even want to think how that would have ended. Maybe what happened was far worse. He swore at me that if I didn't get out of your life immediately and stay away, then he would.

May, I knew how much you loved the man, and I know how much you loved your family. If he left you who else would there be for you to blame but me? So there we'd be. Your family would be broken, and that special bond you and I had would be shattered. I couldn't let that happen.

I tried bargaining him out of it. I pleaded with him and swore I'd never argue with him again, but he'd have none of it. I finally broke down and agreed to the banishment but not before making him promise that he would never leave you. Ever.

So there it is. Honey, I loved you so much I chose to have you think of me as a bad guy this way rather than have you think I broke up your marriage. It's been a bitter daily pill to swallow all these years, believe me.

With your mother gone I just buried myself in my work. That's about all I let myself think about day and night. That is until I found Kane.

Remember how much you and I loved dogs and how much fun we had with Pepper when you were little? Well, a neighbor lady's collie had pups, and when I first laid eyes on that litter, I just had to have one. In fact, I picked Kane out of all the other pups on that first day. I'd go over to my neighbor's place every day and spend hours holding him and playing with him and making sure the other pups didn't crowd him out of getting his fair share of his mother's milk.

As soon as he was weaned, I even talked her into letting me take him home to live with me a few days earlier than he should have.

That dog has filled a void like nothing else could. With you and your mother and the kids gone, Kane has been the most important thing in my life. He's been my best friend and medicine for my soul for several years now.

By now you probably figured out that Kane is a pretty special dog. If all is going as I figure it will, he will be a tremendous help in raising Ben. I only wish that I could be there to see it.

Now that you've learned the truth I hope you'll think a little better of me. I lived up to my end of the bargain, and now it's left to Paul to hold up his end.

That's about all I guess except I expect you to see that Kane knows every day how much you love him. Give him a hug and whisper in his ear how much I love him too. He'll hear you, and he'll understand.

Know that I love you all and please don't any of you forget me.

With love,

Dad

On the envelope in hurried handwriting was a message:

I know you'll never forgive me for my betrayal of you and your family.

I am ashamed for what I have done and hope that I can receive some small amount of forgiveness by returning this letter which I took from your father's box. The envelope did not contain the information I was looking for, but it does contain something that will be of great value to you.

Please let Elizabeth know that I still love her in spite of my greed and cowardice.

I'm sorry.

Nick

Paul was in the den reading the newspaper in front of the large window that overlooked his fields when May approached him and silently tossed the envelope and its contents in his lap. She stood beside him, arms crossed, as he read the letter and when he had finished he dropped it back into his lap and began rubbing his eyes warily.

"That's not quite the way I remember it happening," he said.

May, making a valiant effort to control her building anger, pulled up a bench and sat next to him. Her hands were folded in an attempt to conceal the fact that they were trembling.

"No?" she asked. "What's your recollection of events?"

Paul didn't answer for a long time as he attempted to gather the words that would shine a better light on the way events unfolded those many years ago.

"In the first place," he finally said, "you know he never liked me. He was always . . . ."

"Did you tell him he could never see me again or you would leave me?" May interrupted.

"What?" Paul asked, his face flushed. "No! Honey, you know I'd never . . . ."

Suddenly a litany of suspicions, long held but never verbalized, came rushing all together and all at once to the surface of May's consciousness.

"You never wanted children," she interrupted him again. "You tolerated them, but you didn't want them. I had to coerce you. Okay, I'll take responsibility for that but the neglect you've shown Ben . . . ."

May's voice broke, and she looked about to make sure her son wasn't within hearing distance.

"Ever since he was born you treated him with indifference," she continued, barely managing her outrage. "Then when we found out he was autistic . . . ."

"No, honey . . . ." Paul tried weakly to interject.

May threw up a hand to stop him. "When you found out, you completely turned away from him. He might just as well never have existed. He needed you. I . . . we all needed you."

"I didn't know how to deal with it," Paul said, running his fingers through his hair. "I didn't know what to do. Look, I never signed up for this. I was trying to get the winery going and dealing with all that, and I just didn't know what to do. I still don't know. And now, with the possibility of losing everything, I've had a lot on my plate. And listen, we've done so much better without your father around here giving me those looks of disapproval."

"Funny thing," May said, her eyes becoming cloudy. "When I think back on him now, I only remember him trying to help. I only remember him trying to help and you accusing him of interfering."

"But honey," Paul countered, "he was always interfering. He always made me feel like I didn't know what I was doing. Like I couldn't do anything right."

"Threatening to leave me, chasing him away," May said, standing and grabbing the letter and envelope from his lap, "you think you did that right?"

The tears were flowing now as she stuffed the letter back into the envelope. "All these years without him, worrying and wondering what I did wrong to displease him and now, now that he's gone I finally find out he left my life because he loved me. And you sent him away because you loved yourself more."

May stormed to the door and paused there, looking back at her husband, slouched in the chair, the newspaper folded on his lap.

"And don't tell me you didn't sign up for this," May said to him bitterly. "You signed up for it when you asked me to marry you, and it wasn't in the fine print. It's part of what it means to love someone more than you love yourself."

May was prepared to say a lot more, but she suddenly felt it would be worthless to say anything further. She stood looking at him with a combination of pity and scorn and then, after shaking her head, she left the room, closing the door behind her.

In the silence that followed, the newspaper slid from Paul's lap as he cried.

Ben was enjoying a bowl of soup in the kitchen as May passed through. She paused there for a moment, and while she was trying to decide what to do next, feeling frustrated and angry, she spied Kane sitting beside her son. The dog was looking into her eyes with an unmistakable expression of empathy.

She slid down to the floor and embraced his soft, warm coat and held him tight, reflecting on the thought that the dog was all she had left of her father.

It wasn't long after that the telephone rang.

CHAPTER FIFTEEN

May watched through the front screen door as the dark-colored Lexus pulled into the driveway and parked in front of the house. After the representatives of Prometheacorp had called to request a meeting she had called Sally to be with her and now her aunt sat on the sofa behind her, idly stirring a cup of coffee she held in her hand. Elizabeth, who had also been alerted, stood next to her mother, watching through a front window as the visitors arrived. May assumed Paul was still in the den, but she had not seen him since their discussion earlier that day before she received the phone call, and she was not inclined to include him in the discussion.

Upstairs in his bedroom, Ben had heard the car arrive and was starting down the stairs with Kane to join them when his mother stopped him. She asked him to run along to the back of the house to play for a while because they were going to have a "big people" talk.

Ben had no desire to be included in "big people" talk, so he was willing to comply with his mother's wishes and headed toward the back door.

"Kane," May called after him. "Watch him for me."

The collie looked at her before glancing toward the front screen door and then turned to join Ben.

Dawn Elder reached the door first, and she was joined by Matheson and a short, plump, balding man who carried an important looking black briefcase. She was prepared to ring the doorbell when May opened the door to greet them.

"Oh, good morning," Elder said with a broad smile. She had expected a return greeting but when she saw that May did not so much as offer a smile she quickly realized that the task at hand was likely not to be an easy one.

"You're Missus McLaughlin, I presume," Elder guessed.

May nodded.

"I'm Dawn Elder," the executive announced, handing her a business card. "I'm Prometheacorp Assistant CEO, and this is Ken Matheson from our research department and this," she said gesturing to the third visitor, "is Donald Wyndham. May we come in?"

May stood aside to admit them and studied them closely as they passed. Sally invited the three strangers to sit together on the sofa as she moved to a chair on the other side of the room. She introduced herself and Elizabeth as they all took seats.

"Will Mister McLaughlin be joining us?" Elder asked, looking about the room.

Just as May was about to make excuses for her husband Paul entered the room, having heard their arrival.

"These people are from Prometheacorp," May explained to Paul without looking at him. "My father was working on a project for them and for some reason they want to talk to me . . . to us about it though I have no idea why."

Sally noticed that Matheson kept looking throughout the room. He appeared to be searching for something, and she was sure she knew what it was.

"Looking for something, Mister Matheson?" Sally asked.

"I was admiring Missus McLaughlin's excellent taste in decoration," he said, smiling at her.

Sally flashed him a wordless smile that seemed to say, "I'll *bet* that's what you're looking for."

There was a momentary silence in which Elder had expected someone to offer coffee or water, but as no such offer was forthcoming, she decided to get down to business.

"Missus McLaughlin," Elder began, "I'm not sure if you are aware, but when your father died he was in the midst of an extremely important project he was developing for our company."

"He didn't finish it," Sally interrupted. "I'm his sister. He told me."

"Well, with all due respect," Elder continued, "we're not sure that's completely true."

"Who told you that?" Sally asked. "One of your spies?"

"Nick Stanley, maybe?" Elizabeth spoke up.

"Wait a minute," Paul interjected. "I'm not sure what you're all talking about."

"There's no need to talk around this," Matheson said, taking charge. "Missus McLaughlin's father was hired to engineer a computer program that would greatly increase human intelligence. I'm sure we don't have to tell you the value of such a product."

"Ken," said Wyndham in an attempt to interrupt.

Matheson waved him aside and continued. "We have evidence he may have implanted a computer chip in his dog, the dog you inherited when he died."

"What?" Paul said with disbelief, looking toward May. "You know, that makes sense. Kane is probably the smartest damned dog . . . ."

"Shut up and keep out of this!" May yelled at him suddenly in a tone that surprised both Elizabeth and Sally.

Paul looked at her with bewilderment.

"Look," Matheson started again. "We don't know for sure if he experimented on this dog but if he did and if it turns out he was successful, then legally the dog is the property of Prometheacorp."

"You'll take that dog away from here over my dead body!" May declared.

"Missus McLaughlin," Elder said in a calming voice, trying to win her over. "This can all be answered very quickly. Just let Mister Matheson make a very quick examination of the dog and if he determines there's nothing there, then . . . there's nothing there, and we'll be out of your hair immediately."

"You can be out of our hair right now," May angrily replied. "*Without* examining the dog."

"Hold on, May," Paul said, raising his voice over hers. Turning to the three people on the sofa he asked, "If it turns out the dog does have this thing, and you decide he's your property, wouldn't we be entitled to some kind of compensation?"

"Shut up, Paul!" May yelled at him again.

"Dad!" Elizabeth exclaimed in disbelief.

Wyndham was uncomfortable now, but he gave a slight nod. "We can work something out, I'm sure."

"How much are we talking about?" Paul asked as May uttered a disapproving moan.

"Why don't you let me make a quick examination?" Matheson asked.

Before anyone could respond, Ben suddenly rushed into the room from the backyard, singing "I Am the Walrus" at the top of his lungs.

May yelled at him to leave the room, and Elizabeth hastily grabbed his shoulders preparing to herd him to the backyard, but at that moment Matheson abruptly sprang to his feet. There, behind the boy stood Kane. Everything at that moment came to a sudden standstill until Wyndham spoke.

"Listen, everyone," he said. "We can return with legal authority to examine the dog, or we can quickly get this over with now. If we find evidence of the microchip we'll sit down and talk and yes, Mister McLaughlin, it could prove to be financially rewarding to you and your family. Either way, and I'm sorry to be assertive, we will gain permission."

"Wait, May," Sally said, taking command of the situation. "What does this examination consist of?"

Wyndham turned to Matheson for an answer.

"A few basic commands to begin with," Matheson replied. "There is one other -uh- basic approach, but let's try testing the dog with commands first."

"Alright," said Sally giving a quick wink to May, unseen by the others. "Go ahead."

Matheson nodded his acknowledgment of her approval and started toward Kane. Ben quickly put his arms around Kane's neck.

"That should be close enough right there," Sally cautioned.

Though not happy with the limitation, Matheson stopped and studied the dog a moment. Panting, Kane stared ahead as if oblivious to the professor.

With one finger extended, Matheson's arm shot out toward the dog and pointed to the ground.

"SIT!" he commanded loudly.

The dog's position and demeanor remained unchanged.

A slight smile appeared at the corner of Sally's lips as she cast a knowing glance in May's direction.

"Please ask the boy to stand away from the dog," Matheson requested.

Paul eagerly called out to Ben. "Step away from Kane for a moment, son. Just for a moment. It's OK."

Ben ignored his father.

"It's all right," Sally said to him very soothingly. "We just want to show the smart man here all the tricks Kane knows. Just for a second, sweetheart."

Ben looked curiously up at her smiling face, then back at Kane. Something in her manner reassured him, and he went to her. Kane started to follow, but Sally stopped him and moved him back a few steps to stand alone in the middle of the room.

Before Matheson could issue another command, the dog sat awkwardly, his eyes on Ben.

"My," Sally remarked. "That was certainly a prompt response."

"You know perfectly well that was not in response to my command," Matheson said curtly. He turned back to the dog and then asked, "Can you make him stand up again?"

"Sure," Sally said. Approaching Kane, she placed her hands under his stomach and moved him to a standing position. As soon as she removed her hands, he slid back down to the floor, and it took a couple of attempts before she managed to persuade him to remain in an upright position.

"Now," Matheson addressed the dog after Sally had stepped back. "SIT!"

When there continued to be no response, Matheson issued the command several more times, each time a little louder.

"He probably heard that," Sally said sarcastically.

A slight realization dawned on Matheson, and he gave his associates a knowing glance. As he studied the dog to determine his next move, Kane suddenly plopped down to the floor on his side, lifted his hind leg and proceeded to lick his testicles.

"How much did you say you folks paid to develop that microchip?" Sally asked over Elizabeth and May's laughter.

A disgusted frown covered Matheson's face, but he quickly transformed it to a forced smile.

Slowly moving toward Kane, extending the back of his hand before him as an offering for the dog to sniff, he began to softly vocalize words of assurance as he approached.

"Good dog," he said. "Good, good boy."

Kane simply watched him, panting heavily. When Matheson was close enough to touch him, the dog began licking his hand as Matheson continued to utter words of comfort and in time he moved his hand to the top of the dog's hip and began scratching him at the base of his tail.

Slowly, Matheson reached into his coat pocket with his free hand and withdrew a small metal box. Laying it gently on the floor he managed to open the lid using one hand, and from it, he slowly pulled a syringe, whose needle was already in place.

At the first sight of the syringe, Ben erupted in an ear-piercing scream. Rushing to Matheson, he gave him a strong shove which caught him off balance and threw him back on his posterior, dropping the syringe to the floor. Still screaming, Ben wrapped his arms around Kane's neck and swiftly pulled him away from the stranger as Elizabeth and May rushed to comfort him.

Sally stood up with her hands on her hips.

"I think that tells you all you need to know about the dog's intelligence level, Mister Matheson," she said to the man on the floor as he quickly retrieved his syringe. "It probably also gives you a pretty good notion as to where we stand on removal of this dog. Oh, sorry about all that dog hair on your jacket there. He's shedding a lot right now."

Elder and Wyndham stood, issuing a flood of apologies as Matheson pulled himself to his feet.

As Ben's cry resolved itself into a quiet whimper, Elizabeth escorted him from the room along with Kane.

"We'll be in touch," Wyndham said, handing Paul his business card. "If you need to get ahold of us before then you may contact me at this number or by email."

May grabbed the card from Paul's hand and ripped it up, tossing the pieces into Wyndham's face.

"We won't," she assured him.

Wyndham started to say something else, but Sally interrupted him.

"Don't let the door hit you in the butt on your way out," she told the visitors with false friendliness as she opened the door and stood waiting for them to exit.

Saying nothing further, Elder led the way from the house, followed by her companions.

On their way back to office headquarters, Elder at the wheel, she offered her appraisal of the meeting.

"Well," she said, "I don't know about you, but that dog seemed pretty stupid to me."

"I'd say he was uncannily stupid," Matheson answered with a slight smile from the back seat, reaching into his pocket and retrieving the metal box.

"Are you being sarcastic?" Wyndham asked.

"I've seen enough animal behavior in laboratory tests to recognize genuine intelligence," Matheson replied, "and I believe that what we just witnessed was a clever performance delivered with all the wit and intelligence of a human being."

"We'll need a lot of experts to back up that statement in court," Wyndham said shaking his head.

"Not at all," said Matheson. "DNA will prove our case."

"DNA?" Wyndham remarked with surprise. "You can't determine intelligence from DNA. Can you?"

"As it turns out, we have reports and experimental results from Sam Crisp's early work on the project," Matheson informed him. "Before he developed his microchip he assigned a team to identify a method to measure intelligence through DNA. Many scientists believe this may be possible. Our people did it. Your job will be to persuade a judge to allow us to determine if the chip has actually been implanted in the dog. The DNA will tell us if it worked."

"Before we go to the judge," Matheson said worriedly, "we're going to have to have pretty strong evidence of that dog's intelligence. How in hell are we going to get DNA? That family won't let us near that animal."

"We don't need to," Matheson intoned ominously. "I have all we need."

Looking over his shoulder in the front seat, and from her line of sight through the rearview mirror, Wyndham and Elder observed Matheson as he removed large portions of dog hair from his sleeve and carefully placed the strands in the metal container next to the syringe.

CHAPTER SIXTEEN

The gate in front of the small, private kennel stood open as Paul guided his car through and on to the circular driveway before the house in which Jim Bodie, the kennel owner, resided.

Ben sat uncomfortably next to his father in the front seat while Kane watched from the back. Paul had told May that he wanted to spend the morning with the boy, just the two of them together before he left for his work deployment in a few days. She asked where he was taking him.

"Oh, I don't know," he said evasively. "I figure we'll just drive around and stop wherever our fancy takes us." Leaning down to Ben he added, "And there just may be a big surprise in store if he's a good boy!"

May's icy attitude toward Paul since their encounter a week ago remained unchanged, and it was with considerable indifference that she nodded her approval.

Paul attempted to persuade Ben to leave Kane behind but when it became evident that they wouldn't be separated he, at last, gave in but he did insist that his son sit in the front seat with him rather than sit in the back with the dog. Ben sullenly complied as Paul considered that the outset of their "fun day together" had not begun as amicably as he would have preferred.

As soon as the car had pulled from the McLaughlin driveway onto the main highway, it was evident that this was not going to be just a casual cruise about the countryside. Even Ben sensed that his father was headed someplace specific and when he asked where they were going he was only told, "You'll see." In anticipation of a surprise, Ben studied the large sign by the entrance that read "Rockyridge Kennels" with substantial interest and, in particular, the illustration beneath which depicted a rough collie in full stride.

"Now listen," Paul said to Ben as he stopped his car in the driveway and turned off the ignition. "This is the big surprise I told you about, but you're going to have to leave Kane in the car while you go with me to see what the surprise is."

Ben started to open his mouth to protest loudly, but his father immediately stopped him.

"We'll leave all the windows rolled down," Paul said firmly, "but Kane isn't allowed to go in here. You're going to have to leave him for just a few minutes if you want to see the surprise."

With a frown on his face, Ben angrily stepped from the car and stood staring at the ground, his arms folded across his chest. Kane watched as Paul took his son by the hand and guided him past the front lawn and up to the front door of the house.

Before they could push the front doorbell, Jim Bodie, a paunchy man in his sixties sporting a baseball cap, swung wide the door and extended a warm and friendly greeting.

"Looking for a dog, huh?" Bodie asked.

"Well," replied Paul, glancing at Ben, "I'd kind of hoped it would be a surprise for Ben here."

Bodie apologized profusely for the gaffe and Paul explained his impending departure and how he hoped to give his son a parting gift.

"Uh huh," Bodie said. "Well, there's a few things we need to know about each other, but I do have some pups available.

Come on over to the kennels and let me introduce you to some of them."

Bodie led them to a cool, spacious, concrete floor structure which housed several roomy wire enclosures, each with a doorway leading outdoors to a grass-covered run. Several adult rough collies greeted them with wagging tails and friendly barks as they walked the length of the building past the enclosure gates toward the nursery at the far end. A young girl whom Bodie introduced as one of his kennel help was in the process of tidying one of the enclosures with cleaning equipment and a watering hose.

"You're in luck," Bodie explained as they walked. "Collies are a little hard to come by right now, especially here in California. They just aren't as popular as they were back in Timmy and Lassie's day," he said.

"I found that out," Paul said with exasperation. "I did a lot of searching before I found you. Why is that?"

Bodie stopped by one of the enclosures, opening the gate and extended a hand to a happy tri-colored dog who eagerly accepted his attention.

"Well, it's a number of reasons," he explained, "some good, some maybe not so much so. For one thing, when most families go to look for a dog these days most of them look to adopt from a shelter or a rescue. That's the good thing, but as a result, there's not as many purebred breeders. A lot of laws get passed to restrict the puppy mills from operating. That's another good thing, but unfortunately, some of those laws and restrictions make it difficult for responsible breeders to operate. Not that there's not some idiot breeders out there trying to make money off the latest dog fad, but there's a lot of idiot owners too. I'd hate to see laws get passed that'd make it impossible for a good family to own a dog because of a few bad apples just as I hate to see good breeders forbidden to breed because of a few bad ones.

"People got the idea that collies are hard to take care of, but they aren't if you can spare the time to give 'em plenty of exercise every day and a good brush once in a while. That, and a lot of love."

"By the way," Bodie said, eyeing Paul as he closed the gate on the dog he had been petting and resumed walking, "you're not one of those idiot owners, are you? 'Cause if you are, I won't do business with you. Most of the pups in my litters are already spoken for by other breeders and show people so I don't get too many available for pets but I'll send one to a happy home any chance I get. I'm not in this just to win a bunch of blue ribbons. Happy dogs mean a lot more to me."

Paul assured him that the dog would receive the best of care.

Stopping at a pen slightly larger than the rest located at the far end of the kennel, Bodie opened the gate and stepped inside, gesturing for Ben to follow. Not sure what to expect, the boy cautiously complied as the gate closed behind him, leaving Paul outside the enclosure.

Giving a soft whistle, Bodie called out, "Chloe! Come on girl! Bring your kids with you!"

It only took a moment for the happy, sweet-tempered sable-merle mother to come running into the interior enclosure from the opening that led outside. She was quickly followed by five bouncy, eight week old balls of fluff and fur all falling over one another in their eagerness to be the first.

"Not afraid of dogs, are you?" Bodie asked as the pups surrounded Ben, jumping up on his leg, some pulling at his trousers. Ben shook his head.

Reaching down, Bodie grabbed one pup, smaller than the rest, who was busy attempting to nurse his mother but each time he was about to reach his objective she would move, throwing him off balance.

"Try this one on for size," Bodie said with a big smile, handing the pup to Ben.

As the puppy wiggled, Ben accepted the perky bundle and held it up to look into its face. The pup licked his nose, eliciting a giggle.

"How'd you like to have him as your very own?" Bodie asked Ben. "How would you like him to be your dog?"

Ben, suddenly and without warning, dropped the puppy to the ground. The distance was not great, and the other littermates broke the pup's fall, avoiding any harm.

"No. I have a dog," Ben said, turning and exiting the gate.

"Wait, Ben!" Paul shouted, grabbing him as he started to run from the nursery.

"I don't want another dog! I don't need another dog! I have Kane! I want Kane!" Ben yelled as he squirmed to free himself from his father's grasp.

"You didn't tell me you had a dog already," Bodie interrupted. "Is this some kind of replacement dog you're looking for?"

"Yes," Paul irritably replied.

At that moment all of the dogs in the kennel started barking frantically, but it wasn't the boy's activity that had excited them.

Ben abruptly stopped squirming and stood perfectly still. There, standing before him was Kane, unmoving but ready to intervene if needed.

"Is that your dog?" Bodie asked.

"That's Kane," Ben replied. Finally pulling away from his father's clutches, he ran to his dog. Kneeling next to him, he buried his face in his coat.

"Looks to me like you've already got the perfect dog right there," said Bodie. "Why in hell are you looking for a replacement?"

"I . . . ," Paul began, "I've been offered a lot of money for him. A *lot* of money. My family's welfare may depend on it."

"Your family's welfare," Bodie said eyeing him suspiciously, "or yours?"

"I'll find a dog somewhere else, thank you," Paul replied angrily, preparing to move.

"Hold on a moment," Bodie said. "How much money are you talking about? I'll tell you if it's a fair price."

Paul stopped a moment, debating with himself whether to tell him.

"About a million," he finally revealed.

"Dollars? Somebody offered you a million dollars for that dog?" Bodie said with amazement. "Who on God's green earth would offer that much money for one dog?"

"It's . . . a big company," Paul reluctantly answered. "Prometheacorp."

128

Bodie thought for a moment. "That's the big pharmaceutical outfit, isn't it? What do they want with the dog? A mascot?"

Paul didn't respond.

Suddenly it occurred to Bodie. "Experiments. They want him for experiments! But why *this* dog?"

"He's . . . special," Paul said, wishing to get away. "Look, just never mind. I'll get another dog somewhere else."

"Huh-uh," responded Bodie. "Not if I can do anything about it. Don't try looking in this state for a collie because I'll be getting the word out to all the other breeders not to sell to you. Now get lost before I turn all my dogs loose on you. Collies aren't known to be aggressive, but if I tell 'em to they'd probably be willing to make beef jerky outta you!"

Paul needed no further encouragement as he rushed toward his car with Ben and Kane.

The trip home was made in silence. Driving at an excessive speed fueled by anger, Paul stared straight ahead at the road while Ben sat in the back seat with Kane, sulking. When they arrived home, the boy jumped from the car before it had come to a complete stop, disregarding his father's admonition. Kane was close behind.

Ben's attitude did not go unnoticed by May when he brushed by her as he passed, running up the stairs. Catching him by the shoulder mid-flight, he squirmed in her grasp as she sought to learn the reason for his behavior. Coming from her bedroom, Elizabeth joined them on the stairs.

"Ben?" his mother asked. "What's going on? What's wrong?"

"I can explain," Paul said from the foot of the stairs.

Turning from them he seated himself in the large chair nearby and drew a deep breath as he ran his fingers through his hair. The other family members waited for him to continue. Kane stood nearby, watching him.

"Ben," his father called. "Come here, boy. Please."

His son was reluctant, but after his mother nudged him, he grudgingly crossed the room to stand before his father, refusing to look at him. May and Elizabeth descended to the foot of the stairs and waited by Kane.

"You remember the people who were here the other day to talk to us about Kane?" Paul asked of Ben..

"They want to cut Kane open!" Ben suddenly yelled.

"Oh, I don't think . . . ," Paul struggled to find another way to explain. "Son, those people are doing some very important work. They want to help people."

"Rich people," Ben shot back.

"Sounds like Ben has considerable insight into the situation," Elizabeth joined in.

Paul cast her a disapproving look as he continued. "There's a lot of money. More money than you can ever imagine. It's very important, and they need Kane so they can finish their work."

"They can't have Kane! He belongs to me! They can't have him! You can't make me give him to them! They're bad people!" Ben was yelling again.

Paul tried his best to calm him.

"No, listen," he said. "I don't think they're bad people.

"I think they're bad people," Elizabeth said softly.

Paul continued, choosing to ignore his daughter's remark. "I don't expect you to understand at your age Ben, but someday, when you've grown up, you'll understand. Those people want to give us a lot of money for Kane. A *lot* of money."

"No!" Ben shouted, running to Kane and throwing his arm around him.

Paul stood from his chair. "Ben, it will be so much money I won't have to go away, and they're going to get you a new doctor, a special doctor to . . . to help you. It will make everything so much easier for all of us, and we'll find you another dog even better than Kane. You'll see . . . ."

Ben lowered his voice and speaking succinctly, he declared, "I don't want that money. I don't care how much it is. There isn't enough money to buy Kane, and I won't let them take him!"

Suddenly screaming, he turned and bolted past his mother and sister, Kane swift on his heels as he ran upstairs to his bedroom. He slammed the door behind him.

"You don't understand, Ben," Paul called after him. "We *have* to do this!"

"*We* don't have to do anything of the sort," May said calmly as she walked toward him. "Kane is part of my father's estate, and I'm the only one with the authority to sell him."

"May!" Paul exclaimed with a laugh of disbelief. "They're offering a million dollars, and I talked to a lawyer. He thinks we might even get three times that amount. Can you imagine?"

His wife was staring back at him with an expressionless face.

"He has no conception of how much money that is and what it means," Paul continued, nearly choking with emotion. "It's for his own good, for *all* our own good. We can't throw this away just because a nine-year-old little boy wants to keep a dog."

May turned and looked toward the top of the stairs in a moment of contemplation.

Turning back to her husband, she held out her hand.

"Give me your phone," she said to him. "Let me talk to them."

At first uncertain, Paul fished his mobile phone from the hip pocket of his trousers and searched his call history before handing it to May.

"That's Wyndham's direct line," he indicated. "He's waiting for our call."

May glanced toward Elizabeth who stood leaning against the banister at the foot of the stairs. She gave her daughter a quick wink as she waited for her call to be answered.

"Good afternoon, Mister Wyndham," May spoke into the phone. "This is May McLaughlin calling."

"Well, good morning," Wyndham's voice could be heard to reply. "I had expected to hear from your husband."

"Yes," May said smiling in her husband's direction, "well, as I'm sure my attorney would advise you, my husband has no legal standing in this matter. My father's will left the dog to me."

"Of course," Wyndham acknowledged. "I only thought that he was acting on behalf of the family, you included. I hope he conveyed to you our generous offer."

"I'm sorry if you were misled, Mister Wyndham," she replied. "In fact, the decision is actually not mine to make either. The dog belongs to my son, Ben."

"The boy?" the voice at the other end of the line said in disbelief. "You're going to allow your young son to make a decision this important? Missus McLaughlin, perhaps your husband didn't explain to you. We're offering you one million dollars for the dog and all medical expenses pertaining to treatment for your son's autism. Are you certain . . . ."

"Couldn't be more certain," May replied as she watched Paul drop into the chair.

Wyndham replied with silence and May was prompted to call out his name to make sure he was still on the line. Finally, he responded.

"Please understand," he said in a slow and steady voice. "We believe that the microchip your grandfather developed for us is presently operating inside the dog. In fact, a DNA sample we obtained has proven conclusively . . . ."

"Oh, you can have your stupid microchip," May interrupted with false friendliness.

"I'm afraid it's not that simple," Wyndham explained, tension growing in his voice. "In order to understand how the microchip functions, we must study it in its present operational state. We need to understand how it is connected and the effect it is having on the dog's brain. Missus McLaughlin, legally the program and microchip belongs to Prometheacorp and, by extension, the experimental animal to which it is connected. We have consulted our legal team, and they concur that we are within our rights to claim ownership of the dog. Now we have no obligation to compensate you in any amount, but we understand the attachment the boy has for the dog . . . ."

"No," said May cutting him off. "You have no idea of the attachment the boy has for the dog. Have you ever owned a dog yourself? Did you bond with it or was it just something that lived in the backyard all day and spent its time endlessly barking out of boredom?"

Wyndham allowed for a long silence before continuing. "Listen very carefully. I'm going to make this final offer. I will make this offer only once, and if you do not accept it immediately, we'll take this to court and let a judge decide. Two million dollars. That's our final offer."

"Wow!" May exclaimed and then called out to Elizabeth. "Did you hear that? Two million dollars!"

May called up the stairs to Ben.

"Ben! Ben! Come here! Quick!" she shouted.

Ben walked slowly out of his room and looked down the stairs toward his mother, a frown covering his face.

"Ben," his mother continued. "They want to give you two million dollars to take Kane away and cut him up and look inside of him and stuff. What do you think? You know how much money that is, don't you?"

"Missus McLaughlin," Wyndham tried to cut her off.

"How much money will you sell Kane for?" May asked Ben.

"Not even a million *cadrillion* billion!" Ben yelled angrily. He slammed the door to his room behind him, loud enough for Wyndham to hear.

"Not even a *cadrillion* billion?" May gasped.

"You would be well advised to have your attorney contact me at his earliest convenience," Wyndham replied with finality. "With the legal resources available to us you may very well find that your legal expenses will be far in excess of several 'cadrillion' and in the end, the dog will still be declared our property. Goodbye, Missus McLaughlin."

CHAPTER SEVENTEEN

Barely three days after Prometheacorp made its final offer Kane could be heard at the front door barking loudly at a stranger who stood outside preparing to knock. The young, bearded man dressed casually in rumpled clothing that might have been slept in carried a messenger bag over his shoulder, and he was smiling at Kane, speaking to him softly in an effort to curtail the clamor.

Ben was staying even closer to Kane these days and was the first to rush to his dog, pulling him away from the door as he attempted to move him upstairs. Paul was in town taking care of legal matters in anticipation of his deployment to Afghanistan, but May and Elizabeth responded to the visitor as they called out to Kane to stop his barking.

Sizing up the stranger through the front door screen, May folded her arms and shook her head.

"You don't look like a Prometheacorp stooge," she said to the man.

"No, I'm not," replied the stranger whose demeanor betrayed a shy nature.

"My name is John Hadley," he said, fishing an official-looking credential from his coat pocket and displaying it to May. "I maintain an online journal called the Hadley Report. Maybe you've seen it?" he asked nervously.

"That's not a press credential," May said suspiciously, as she eyed the document he held.

"Well no, it's not really a press credential as such," Hadley said with embarrassment as he shoved it back in his pocket. "The twenty-first-century press is all owned by huge corporations, but I report my stories online, so I don't answer to any moneyed interests. I'm an investigative journalist. Maybe one of the last."

"I think I've heard of you," Elizabeth said, joining her mother.

"The Hadley Report," he responded eagerly to the recognition. "May . . . May I come in?"

May stood for a moment considering the request before looking in her daughter's direction. Elizabeth shrugged. That was good enough for May, and she opened the screen door to admit the visitor.

"Have a seat," she said, pointing to the sofa. "Water? Tea? Soft drink?"

"Thank you, no," he said unslinging his bag as he sat.

He noticed Kane and Ben who were standing nearby eyeing him curiously.

"Don't worry," he said holding up a hand toward Ben. "I'm not here to take your dog away. I'm on your side."

"Okay," May said, feeling her impatience grow. "What do you want from us?"

Reaching into his bag, Hadley pulled a large computer tablet and turned on the power.

"I have . . . ," he said, struggling for a word, ". . . a friend on the inside who's been willing to share some insider information regarding the goings-on at Prometheacorp. I wouldn't be surprised if you haven't read my reports, probably not a great many have, but let's just say that a big company who manufactures products that can save lives and then prices those products far beyond any reasonable profit margin, well, it's just plain greed, nothing else. It's the sort of thing I fight against. With words, of course."

"What about development costs?" Elizabeth asked, seating herself nearby. "Isn't that the old alibi?"

"Sure," Hadley replied, "but the only expense that ever goes up is executive pay and bonuses for the CEO. Development expenses generally remain the same year after year regardless of how many new miracle drugs they deliver to the world at outlandish prices."

Taking a breath, he attempted another approach. "I'm sorry for getting on a soapbox but as you can tell I feel pretty passionate about this stuff."

"Then I'll ask again," May repeated, "what do you want from us?"

"I want to break the news about the Mastermind Project," he replied.

"The what?" May asked.

"Well," Hadley continued, "that's what they call it, the computer chip your father developed for them. It's designed to increase the intelligence of any person . . . ," he nodded toward Kane, ". . . or dog in which it has been planted. That's great of course except, as your father eventually realized, despite the peanuts it would cost to manufacture and implant, the plan is to market it at an astronomically exorbitant price. Only the extremely wealthy will benefit, probably enabling them to figure more ways to become even wealthier. As usual with Prometheacorp and the like, it's really not about benefiting mankind. It's about more money for the investors. In short, Missus McLaughlin, Kane is presently the most valuable creature on the face of the earth."

Ben's fingers tightened on the rough about Kane's neck.

"And in case you had any doubts," Hadley continued, "they will do *anything* they can to take possession of your dog, and once they have him they will do anything to your dog including vivisection to unlock the secrets of the chip implanted in him."

"Ben," May called to her son. "Please take Kane upstairs and play in your room."

The boy wasn't about to move, however, and he remained firmly seated. He didn't know the meaning of the word "vivisection" but it sounded deadly, and he wanted to know more.

"If a program like Mastermind is going to exist," Hadley resumed, "it doesn't deserve to be in the hands of fat cats like Prometheacorp. Now, I know they've already served you with a lawsuit . . . ."

"This morning," May nodded.

He shook his head. "When are you scheduled to appear?"

"Three days from now. Monday," she replied. "Our family attorney is on his way here now to talk about it."

"I'll bet he is," Hadley said sarcastically. "And I'll bet he has a tidy sum of cash already stuck away somewhere in unmarked bills compliments of the generous folks at Prometheacorp."

"Well, that wouldn't surprise us," Elizabeth said. "When he called us this morning he sounded a dire warning that a war with Prometheacorp couldn't be won. He was recommending we consider a sale price."

"Okay," Hadley jumped in, "Forget about your family attorney. He's going to try to keep his hooks in you 'cause he won't want to have to return Prometheacorp's money. I'll refer you to a lawyer, and he'll defend you for free. Don't thank me now. We need to start a media blitz ASAP, big corporation trying to take away autistic boy's dog, that sort of thing. All the social media sites will love it."

Hadley was typing frantically on his tablet.

Elizabeth narrowed her eyes. "What's in this for you?"

"Don't you think being the journalist who reminded big pharma about the need for a little humanity is enough?" He stopped typing a moment and pushed his computer away.

"I had a kid brother," he said, briefly glancing at Ben. "He had a rare disease. Prometheacorp manufactured a medicine that could have helped him, but my family couldn't afford it, and they wouldn't budge on the price. My brother died. We sued. We lost. I was a reporter for *The New York Times,* and I wrote a pretty damaging report about it. Prometheacorp sued me. I lost, and I got fired. I owe them."

"If you take them on again," Elizabeth warned, "You could lose again, Big."

He sat in silence for a moment before resuming his typing. "Yeah, well I practically live out of my car these days. It needs new brakes. They can have it. Listen, we've got to get moving on this."

"Wait," May interrupted. "I'm not sure . . . . I don't know if it would be good for Ben to be in the spotlight like that."

"Missus McLaughlin," Hadley said, shaking his head, "it's already too late for that, and you can thank Prometheacorp.

They won't want the public to know they're taking away a kid's dog but that's gonna be what the public picks up on when this goes to court. They're going to try to paint you as a crazy family who refused an astronomical sum of money to help your autistic son and all they're asking in return is the privilege of studying an insignificant dog."

He stopped a moment and then resumed his typing.

"Gotta get the animal rights guys in on this too," he added.

May sat beside her son and attempted to hug him, but he was resistant as usual. Instead, he hugged Kane. Hadley noticed the interaction.

"This is going to be tough," he spoke to her in a soft voice. "You're going to become national, probably international celebrities and no matter how hard we fight, in the end, you may lose anyway. You should be prepared for that."

"I know," May said.

She rubbed the area behind Kane's ear as a tear streaked down her cheek.

CHAPTER EIGHTEEN

The social network was suddenly aflame.

With headlines ranging from "Greed Grabs Autistic Boy's Collie" to "Big Corporation vs. A Boy and His Dog," the vast majority of commentators were unequivocally on the McLaughlin's side. There were a few detractors of course, who maintained that the family had no business standing in the way of medical progress just for one dog and one boy and that all Americans have the right to charge as much as they like for products they own but such comments were fiercely shouted down the way the internet can manage to do so thoroughly.

The news media, too, picked up on the story and they clamored for interviews. Sally took temporary leave of her part-time veterinary work to move in with the family and assumed responsibility for fielding the media requests. Elizabeth was appointed responsibility for Ben and Kane and for keeping them away from the media madness that continued to build. May was family spokesperson and final decision-maker, while Hadley remained in constant contact as advisor along with three idealistic young attorneys who came to the family's defense pro bono.

Paul remained incommunicado to all but his family and to them he spoke rarely and briefly. He knew he was on the wrong side of the tide of opinion and though he still believed he was right, he recognized the futility of resisting. Instead, he quietly prepared for his work deployment, a topic that was not lost on the media and the internet. Prometheacorp was not just taking away a little autistic boy's dog, it was taking away a dog who belonged to a little boy whose father was leaving for Afghanistan, leaving behind a schoolteacher wife burdened with debt to do battle with a ruthless monster in order to protect her family.

And all of this had erupted in only one twenty-four hour period.

Prometheacorp had its work cut out for them. During their first court appearance, their attorneys appealed for an expedited ruling, citing concerns that the family might attempt to hide the dog and that the longer Prometheacorp's scientists were refrained from examining him, the greater the chance that important information might be lost as there was no guarantee as to the durability of the disputed object. The agreement Sam had signed was presented as proof that the microchip planted within the dog, because it was now *part* of the dog, made them the dog's legal owners.

The McLaughlin's attorneys' argument was simpler: the dog and the microchip were not one.

It was on that distinction that Judge Davenport's decision would hinge, and after accepting the written statements of the two parties, he announced that he would rule in one week. Court was adjourned and scheduled to reconvene the following Monday.

The crowds gathered outside the courthouse were not content with the judge's pronouncements, and because there was no immediate dismissal of the case, there were cries for the impeachment of Judge Davenport, boycotts, sit-ins and even threats of violence. A boy and his dog had become the number one topic of concern across the nation even spilling over into the political arena where representatives and candidates quickly learned that if they did not come out strongly on the side of the McLaughlins they would be well advised to simply express confidence in the American judicial system and leave it at that.

The news of the court hearing was related to Tom Burch in a meeting held in the Prometheacorp boardroom bursting with company staff, attorneys, and advisors, some of which had been procured from outside sources. Each attendee was eager to express an opinion and relate their experience running the vast gauntlet of protestors surrounding Prometheacorp headquarters.

A simple hand raised by Burch promptly silenced the group, and Wyndham was allowed to sum up, the details of the court session, concluding with the opinion of both he and his fellow attorneys that the ruling could go either way but in their opinion was weighted in Prometheacorp's favor.

"In that case," Burch concluded, "there is nothing more that can be done on the legal side for the week to come. Now, as to the public relation side . . . ."

There was a sudden torrent of opinion as everyone spoke up at once. Again Burch held up a hand, and the voices were immediately silenced.

"Statements have been issued to all media," he continued, "reminding the American people of the importance of the Mastermind Program not only to the citizens of this country but to all of mankind. Psychologists favorable to our case have issued their expert opinion that the separation of the dog from the boy will have only a minor, temporary and very brief impact on the young man and that the immediate substitution of . . . ," Burch thumbed through the pages of a paper report spread out before him.

" . . . A puppy," Wyndham, sitting nearby coached.

"A puppy," Burch continued as if he had known it all along, "will more than heal any stress the young man may think he is experiencing."

Elder was sitting near her boss, and he nodded toward her as she raised her hand to speak.

"Now," she started, "as to the claims of profit mongering, perhaps we should . . . ."

"That will be all for now," Burch announced, dismissing the crowd in the room. As everyone proceeded to disassemble, he motioned for Wyndham and Elder to remain.

"Look," he said to his two assistants as the door closed behind the last employee to vacate the room, "they can say what they will about the profit issue and most of the criticism will be directed toward me, which is as it should be. The fact is, I don't take these things personally. I was hired to make as much money for our shareholders as I possibly can and in the end that's all that matters. As long as I can do that legally, that's what I'm paid to do. I believe we'll weather this storm and if the Mastermind Program yields the profit I believe it will bring in, it won't matter how sales of our other products fall, and it won't matter what anybody says about this company or about me. I will have done my job. Nothing personal. For now, we've got a shareholders' meeting coming up in San Francisco in two weeks, and if we're victorious in court, we're going to have good news that'll wash away any moral reservations our investors might be harboring. I also want to remind you that there's a leak somewhere in this organization and I want to know who it is. You find out who's leaking and get me that damned dog. The rest will take care of itself."

During the week that followed Burch's pronouncement, it seemed that there was only one topic of conversation throughout the United States and it all centered around a boy and his collie. The McLaughlin family was unable to venture out of their house because of the battery of news reporters, sympathizers and the curious amassed outside their gate waiting for just a glimpse of a family member.

Chuck and Ray were employed by the family not to tend the vineyards but rather to roam the fields, chasing away trespassers and interlopers and the area directly behind the house was the only location where Ben and Kane were allowed outside but only after a thorough sweep of the area had been made. The two men pitched a small tent on a rise in the field and traded shifts night and day to ensure 24-hour surveillance. Even with those precautions drones and long-range photographic lenses were still able to capture images of the two celebrities.

Through his online blog, Hadley attempted to feed the media hysteria with true facts and updates, rejecting the abundant rumors, phony news reports and false claims that proliferated. As the only journalist authorized by the family to disseminate official information on their case, his fingers rarely left the keyboard of his laptop. Aided by a secret "inside source" at Prometheacorp, whom he referred to under the code name Old Yeller, Hadley was privileged to information from both sides of the case, but he refused to be recruited by the major news organizations. Such employment, he vowed, would compromise his principles and would be nothing more than a sell out to the big money interests that controlled all information. He declared that these were the enemies he fought on a daily basis and he insisted that big money versus individual freedom was what this very case was all about.

May strictly limited interviews to one a day and only with what she considered the most reliable news sources. The remote interviews were conducted within the house, but Ben and Kane were never present. Though the family was fearful of the outcome of the legal proceedings, they were eager for the issue to be resolved in order that they might resume their lives.

The boy and his dog were bound together during this period as if one. Ben only had a very vague idea of what all the attention was about, but it seemed to the family that Kane was fully aware of all that was happening and what was at stake and that knowledge made him very nervous.

The family had determined that although he was incapable of human speech the special mentality the dog possessed empowered him with the ability to comprehend what was being spoken. This acumen also appeared to expand the inherent abilities that Kane, like all dogs, already possessed, such as sensitivity to human emotions and social cues, the ability to use an extraordinary sense of smell to perceive and identify things that cannot be seen as well as many others still not fully understood by scientists. The combination of canine and human perception resulted in a unique mentality. The family would often pause to wonder exactly what was going on inside Kane's head but the turmoil swirling about them didn't leave much time for contemplation.

Thursday marked the date of Paul's departure for Afghanistan. Though some of his luggage had already been shipped ahead, one suitcase traveled with him, and he set it near the front door. It was decided that in order to avoid the spectacle they knew his departure would create among the news media, the family would say their farewells at the house and that he would travel by himself to the airport via taxi.

As his ride pulled up in front of the house, the family gathered around Paul awkwardly, and Sally was first to give him a hug and to wish him Godspeed. Elizabeth was next, and with tears in her eyes, she hugged her father long and tightly. When she finally broke her embrace, he turned to his wife and without hesitation, swept her up in his arms and buried his face in her shoulder.

"I've said it before," he whispered in her ear, "but I can't say it enough. I love you so much, and I'm so sorry. For everything. Maybe this break will be good for us, and when I get back we can start fresh, and I can make it up to you. I'm going to try very hard. I promise. Just don't give up on me. Please."

"I promise to do my part to make that happen," May whispered back. "Just be careful and come home soon. I love you."

There were tears in her eyes when he broke the embrace, and he turned quickly so she wouldn't see the tears forming in his own eyes. He was met with the sight of Ben standing nearby, a quizzical look on his face, and Kane, ever present, at his side. Paul approached and knelt before Ben, holding his arms tightly.

"I'm counting on you now, Son, to take care of our family," Paul said to him. "You're the man of the house now, and I know I can rely on you."

"We'll take care of everybody," Ben replied very seriously, "Kane and me."

"I'm sure you will," Paul said, casting a worried look toward Kane. "But remember no matter what happens to Kane, you're strong, and you can cope with anything anybody throws at you. Right?"

"Right," Ben affirmed. "Kane will always be with me. We'll be okay."

Paul wished he could stay longer and that he could prepare Ben for what was likely to be a separation from Kane but now he was out of time and he would have to rush to catch his plane. He gave his son a firm hug before turning to the collie, patting him on his neck.

"Thank you, Kane," he said to him. "Thank you for everything. Goodbye, old fella."

Rising quickly, Paul grabbed the handle of his suitcase, and in an instant, he was gone.

The family remained standing where he left them as a telephone began ringing nearby.

The remainder of the week seemed to drag sluggishly and oppressively by, and the combination of Paul's departure and the dread of Monday's court decision created a dark, low-lying cloud that hung over the inhabitants of the McLaughlin household, casting gloom, stifling conversation, cheerless and depressing.

The dreary attitude of the family was not lost on Ben who, despite Kane's best efforts, was becoming more withdrawn, uncooperative and short tempered. He would often demand that Kane crawl under his bed and command him to lay there quietly for long periods of time believing that if he hid him there, he would not be found. Kane silently and obediently complied, being fully tuned in to Ben's fears.

From under the bed, Kane heard the phone ring at 11:30 on Monday morning. As Elizabeth answered the call from downstairs, Ben wrapped his arms around his knees and buried his face in his lap as he sat on the floor nearby, and a low moan began to rise from his throat first quietly and gradually ever louder as he rocked back and forth.

Kane crawled from under the bed and placed his long muzzle near his boy's cheek, but Ben at first shoved him angrily away and then, almost as quickly, pushed him back under the bed before crawling under after him, grabbing him tightly as he screamed a long, heartrending cry.

CHAPTER NINETEEN

On Tuesday morning, Tom Burch was sitting in a chair on the soundstage of a local television station as make-up was touched up and preparations were made for his first nationally televised interview on the Mastermind issue. Security was tight both inside and outside the facility, and he had been flown in to the studio by helicopter without fanfare in order to avoid encountering the public. There were death threats. Arrests had been made.

Speaking into a camera, Shannon Langley, the morning news celebrity who would be conducting the interview, began.

"It's been less than twenty-four hours since Judge Harrison Davenport passed down his decision that a young autistic boy's collie dog, which has been implanted with a near-miraculous microchip, is considered to be the property of Prometheacorp, a large technology, and pharmaceutical corporation. The decision was based on the argument that the microchip could not operate independently of the dog and therefore the dog and the microchip may be considered as one and that the benefit the microchip might offer to all mankind far outweighs all other considerations. Although an appeal is being filed, there is little hope for a different outcome, and a restraining order has been denied.

"The case has sparked outrage and protests since news of the case became public a week ago and now Prometheacorp faces the daunting challenge of taking possession of the dog, inciting death threats and boycotts.

"This morning, we are joined in studio by Prometheacorp CEO Tom Burch who, for the first time, has agreed to speak with us on the issue. Good morning, Mister Burch."

Burch produced a smile that seemed sincere and humble. "Good morning, Shannon."

"I must ask you," the newswoman began, "how, in the face of almost overwhelming public outrage, your company would dare go forward with your plan to take possession of the dog."

"Well, first let's call 'the dog' by his name because to us he is much, much more than just a dog. His name is Kane and, by the way, Shannon, a more beautiful creature on the face of the earth does not exist. Kane is going to surrender to mankind all of the extremely important secrets he possesses and as tough a decision as it may be for us to separate him from the young man he only recently came to live with, we made the decision knowing full well there may be some who will not understand but we also made that decision knowing in our hearts that everyone, including those shouting most loudly, will soon have the opportunity to live a better life thanks to Prometheacorp. And remember, we only want to study the dog, not kill him." Burch chuckled.

"The question on everyone's mind right now is exactly when the transfer of the dog will take place," Shannon said.

"Well, this has to be handled carefully to make the transition as smooth as possible for Kane's sake," Burch replied. "And for the young man as well. Hopefully, the McLaughlin family and the crowd gathered around their home will cooperate with Judge Davenport's judgment so that this can all be handled peacefully and legally. We'll make a decision sometime during the next few days after conferring with the family."

"Incidentally," Burch added with a big smile, "young Mister McLaughlin isn't going to be left empty-handed. In exchange for willingly placing Kane in our care and to show our gratitude for the responsibility he has demonstrated during the short time the animal has been with him, we think he's going to be genuinely happy when we present him with this little fellow."

At that moment an assistant stepped forward and handed a young Shetland Sheepdog to him. The dog stood uneasily in his lap for only a moment before jumping down to the floor, scampering into the wings of the set, his leash trailing behind him.

Several miles away at the McLaughlin home, Ben was waking from a troubled night's sleep. He kept his eyes tightly closed, wishing the day away.

A ray of bright morning sunlight radiated through a small opening in the bedroom curtains where May had failed to completely draw them together when she tucked him in the night before. It cast a narrow path of light across the floor and onto the bed stopping just short of where Kane lay next to him, watching his boy's every move. Kane had been in the same spot all night as he was every night but this time he had not slept and instead had spent the entire time watching Ben's face, never wavering, never moving until now.

A noise outside prompted Kane to lift his head, tilting it sideways in an effort to hear better as he looked toward the window from which the sound came. Stepping gently off the bed so as not to disturb Ben he quietly walked to the window and placed his front paws on the sill, moving the opening in the curtains aside with his muzzle in order to view the scene outside below.

The crowd he saw was now enormous and filled not only the empty field on the other side of the home but also lined both sides of the road outside the gate as far as the eye could see. Most camped overnight and a generous donor supplied portable toilets and stationed them nearby. Police on motorcycles continually moved slowly up and down the highway, keeping it clear and preventing the crowds from blocking access, and now and then helicopters hovered overhead.

The noise that had drawn Kane to the window was the sound of motorcycle engines as an extensive parade of roaring bikes passed by, the ragged riders revving their engines and flashing raised fists in support of the family. It was just one of several very noisy demonstrations that continually took place since Judge Davenport made his decision.

Ben opened his eyes and called out to Kane, and the dog returned to him, sitting beside the bed and resting his head near his hand, looking up into his face. Ben yawned and rubbed the sleep from his eyes with one hand while he stroked his dog's fur with the other. The crowds outside only bored Ben, and he resented them because of the restrictions they caused to be placed upon him. Hopping from bed, he directed his attention to a plastic dinosaur which lay upon the floor waiting for Ben's hands to give it life.

At mid-morning, May's cell phone rang while she and Elizabeth, sitting on the large front room couch read a handful of newspapers which lay stacked nearby, all of which carried leading articles about Ben and Kane. Nearby, Sally looked up from her laptop computer.

"Sargent Goodwin," May announced to the others as she read the caller identity from the face of her phone. The policeman was in charge of a small group of law enforcement personnel who had been stationed around the area outside the gate to deter intruders and maintain order among the crowd.

"Are they here?" May asked.

Sargent Goodwin was confused. "Are they here?"

"Are they here to take the dog?" May clarified.

"Oh, no," Goodwin replied, "but I could use your influence out here. Could you step outside for just a moment? I think you could help."

With a quizzical look on her face, May crossed the room and opened the front door. Outside she saw Sargent Goodwin standing in the middle of the yard waiting for her. At the gate a group of police were gathered around a group of grizzled men, some wearing bandanas around their heads, some with cowboy hats and all of them dressed in camouflage. Most wore ammunition belts and pistols and nearly all sported assault rifles slung over their shoulder. Behind them sat an imposing looking armored personnel carrier followed by a line of pickup trucks, all displaying American flags.

"I apologize for bothering you," Goodwin said as May approached him. "We've got a group of citizens at the gate who claim to be militia members. Some of them have traveled from out of state to be here and, well, they're managing to make my officers a little uncomfortable. I thought maybe if you could talk to them face to face, maybe encourage them to back down we could diffuse a potential problem before it gets out of hand."

May felt a sickening pain in her stomach. "What do they want?"

"Why don't you let their leader explain?" Goodwin offered, leading her forward to the gate.

May followed and was soon facing a short, bearded man who tossed her a military-style salute and nodded toward her from behind very dark eyewear.

"Good morning to you, Missus McLaughlin," he said with a thick (May thought) affected Southern dialect. "I am Field Commander Burnside of the American Coalition of Citizen's Rights, and I'm honored to inform you that we have been dispatched to this location in order to protect you and your family in this, your time of need. I want to assure you that as long as we are here, there will be no trespassing on these premises by anyone at any time to take illegal possession of anything including your boy's dog. I don't care what branch of the so-called government they claim to be from."

May surveyed the militia members arrayed before her. "Am I to assume your devotion to this cause could include armed confrontation?"

Burnside nodded his head sharply with a little wink of his eye. "If it comes to that, Ma'am, you can be assured we're more than prepared for it."

"Well, listen, Commander Burnside . . . ," May started.

"Field Commander Burnside, Ma'am," he corrected her.

"Okay, listen Mister Burnside," May continued as she felt Her patience waning. "I appreciate your noble effort here, but I'm afraid I'm going to decline your offer. I am under the legal protection of Sargent Goodwin and his men, and I am more than adequately secure and safe. Please pack up your men and your guns and . . . ."

"Ma'am, Ma'am!" Burnside interrupted, holding up a hand to silence her. "With all due respect, these cops here cannot and will not prevent that dog from being taken from these premises, and you know that. Now, in the absence of the head of your household, my men and me are prepared to step in to prevent that from happening even if you yourself are unable or unwilling to do so."

May's mouth opened wide in outrage. ". . . In the absence of the head of my household!"

Preparing to direct a volley of outrage toward Burnside for daring to misrepresent her status of authority over her own household, May was promptly ushered back toward her house by Sargent Goodwin. At the front door, he asked permission to speak with her inside where they were joined by Sally and Elizabeth.

Once inside, May fumed. "The arrogance of that . . . that ass! How am I supposed to get rid of him?"

"You see what we're up against here," Goodwin said apologetically. "We've got to step very delicately. Feelings are running pretty high out there, and someone could easily get hurt, especially when they get here to collect your dog."

"What in the world can I do?" May questioned, raising her hands in frustration.

There was a pause as everyone contemplated their options. Eventually, Sargent Goodwin answered the question.

"I think you probably know the answer to that question," he said.

There was another long interlude of silence as they all allowed his words to sink in.

With an air of surrender, May collapsed in a large chair.

"They'll eventually take him anyway. You do know that," he added.

May nodded woefully as Elizabeth and Sally sat next to her on the arms of the chair doing their best to comfort her.

CHAPTER TWENTY

While Ben and Kane played outdoors at the back of the house under the watchful eye of Chuck and Ray, the McLaughlin household spent the remainder of the morning and a good portion of the afternoon devising a plan for delivering Kane to Prometheacorp headquarters. As loathsome as the decision was, the declaration of the armed militia outside the gate now made it unavoidable.

Getting the dog past the crowd out front was less an obstacle than was the dreaded task of removing Kane from Ben. Suggestion after suggestion was put forth only to be discarded as May, Elizabeth and Sally considered their options. In the end, there seemed no other alternative but to speak to the two of them and simply explain what had to happen and then immediately separate them. It would have to be quick, like pulling a tooth, only infinitely more painful.

Gathering in the front room, their plan finally agreed upon, the three women stood in a circle holding hands, hoping to acquire strength from one another. Ultimately, it seemed there was no strength to be collected because no one had any strength left to give, only tears and despair.

At last, when no one else could make a move to put their plan into action, Sally walked through the kitchen and opened the door leading out back. Ben and Kane were both sitting on the swing together as Chuck squatted nearby watching them while Ray, carrying a sizable stick, patrolled the fields nearby.

Sally tried to call out to Chuck, but her voice stuck in her throat and required a couple of attempts before she could finally make herself heard. Rushing to her, Chuck eyed her suspiciously as she issued instructions to him.

"I need you to do something for me, Chuck," she told him with a hand on his shoulder. "I need you to tell Ben and Kane to come into the house for a moment." Handing him her car keys she continued, "Then I want you to bring around my SUV and park it close to the back door. Keep the engine running. Open the front door and the back door on the driver's side, and leave them open. Will you do that for me?"

Chuck didn't like the sound of it, but he nodded and slowly turned to walk toward the swing while Sally, her head bowed, returned to the house.

Inside, she found the mother and daughter ready to tackle the task at hand, and they stood in silence until Ben and Kane entered, looking up at them with curiosity. With a deep sigh, May walked over to the adjacent door which led to the den and motioned for Ben to join her.

"Ben," she said affecting false cheerfulness, "Your sister and I would like to speak to you for a moment in here, in the den."

Ben didn't move. Elizabeth leaned down to him.

"Remember how Daddy said you were going to have to be the man of the house while he was gone?" Elizabeth asked. "Well, this is one of those times. Mommy and I need your help. Will you come talk to us a moment?"

Ben was reticent but slowly took his sister's hand and followed, though somewhat reluctantly. Kane started to follow but stopped when Sally held her hand up as a signal for him to stay. While the separation seemed at first to be working, Ben suddenly stopped in the doorway and turned back.

"Come on, Kane," he said motioning to the collie. When Kane remained beside Sally, Ben immediately grasped what was taking place. With a quick look into the face of his mother and sister, Ben suddenly shrieked with a sound louder and more heart-rending than any the three women had ever heard before and in a flash Elizabeth and May grabbed the boy and pulled him into the den, closing the door in Kane's face as he rushed forward, too late to follow.

Once inside it took every effort the two women could manage to hold him as he struggled and struck them with his fists attempting to free himself and return to his dog.

May attempted in vain to explain to him that there was no choice but for Kane to voluntarily go with the people that the judge had decided were his owners and how he must be a very strong young man and that would mean sometimes having to deal with very painful decisions and that it was all beyond anyone's control. She tried to impart such wisdom to the boy as Elizabeth kept repeating how much they loved him but all of it was lost on Ben as he violently fought against them all the while repeatedly screeching, "KANE! KANE!"

Meanwhile, Kane was scratching frantically at the door as Ben's anguished cries tore his heart apart. Sally rushed to him and grabbed the rough around his neck, directing him to look into her face.

"Listen to me, Kane!" She shouted to him. "Listen! We don't have much time. I know you can understand what I'm saying, or at least you get the general idea, and I need you to listen closely. This family is in very great danger right now if we don't comply with the court order to turn you over to them. There are men outside with guns who may harm someone if they come here to take you away and that may happen soon. This is the only way we can make this all go away peacefully, and we can only hope and pray that you will understand. I know it's in your nature to do what's best for this family even if it means sacrificing your own safety and right now we're asking you to make a sacrifice. Dammit, this is the toughest thing I've ever had to ask anyone to do, but I'm asking you. Right now. Do this for us. Please come with me. Please!"

She was sobbing now. Kane gave her a soft lick on her cheek as Ben's voice continued to call his name mournfully from the next room.

Gathering her strength, Sally commanded Kane to follow her. Grabbing her purse and a small bag containing laundry from a nearby table she used her other hand to lift a blanket that had been placed across the arm of the couch as she led him toward the back door. Once outside she helped him into the back seat of her SUV that stood waiting, its engine running. She coaxed him onto the floor and covered him with the blanket, urging him to stay very still and quiet. As a final precaution, she emptied the contents of the laundry bag on top of the blanket. The task done, she closed the back door and turned to Chuck, who stood holding the front door. Giving his hand a pat of gratitude she slid behind the steering wheel and closed the door then withdrew her cell phone from her purse and selected a phone number that had been pre-set.

"I'm ready," she said into the phone. "I'm driving around now." Tossing her phone back into her purse she put her vehicle in gear and drove around the building to the front yard.

Dusk was preparing to settle in as she steered her SUV toward the gate where Burnside stood talking to two of his armed cohorts. The sight of Sally's vehicle drew the attention of everyone nearby, and she approached slowly, rolling down only the driver's side window. Gesturing with a friendly wave, she greeted Burnside with a genial smile, rolling to a near stop as he approached. Several police officers stood nearby, but Sergeant Goodwin was not among them.

"Good evening!" Sally called out to Burnside. "Everything under control out here?"

The militant placed his hand on the window in front of her. "Stop the vehicle here, Ma'am," he ordered.

"What's up?" she asked as she brought the SUV to a full stop.

"We're going to need to know where you're going. It's for your protection," he answered her as he tried to look over her shoulder into the back seat. All of the windows behind her were tinted, making it impossible to see through them into the rear from the outside.

"Oh, I've got to check in on my animals at home and then I'm going to pick up some groceries. I'll be back in just a bit." She waved him off and started to accelerate again but was stopped as Burnside placed a hand on her shoulder to stop her.

"Hold on!" he ordered. "We need to inspect the back seat first. For your protection."

"What?" she reacted indignantly. Reaching behind her seat, she grabbed a bra from the pile of laundry scattered over the blanket and dangled it in Burnside's face. "Listen buster, if you think I'm going to let you dig through my dirty laundry, you're going to need more than an assault weapon. In case you didn't notice, the bad guys are trying to get in, not get out. I'll catch you later."

Sally tossed the bra over her shoulder and accelerated suddenly, and Burnside quickly withdrew his hand to avoid the risk of being dragged. The armed militia jumped from the path of her vehicle as she moved down the highway at an alarming speed.

Burnside watched her leave, a suspicious look on his face.

About half a mile down the road Sally observed a police vehicle that had been parked beside the road suddenly pull in front of her as an escort, turning on its red lights. Through the window, she could see Sergeant Goodwin in the passenger's seat, and he waved at her. A second police car pulled out behind her and followed. Breathing a sigh of relief, Sally reached behind the seat and removed the blanket and laundry that had been covering Kane.

"We should be OK now, boy," she told him as he climbed onto the back seat from the floor, "though I'd just as soon our destination was somewhere else."

Kane lay down on the seat and rested his head between his paws. He showed no interest in the scenery passing by.

For her part, Sally tried to block the deep depression she was feeling. She cried as she considered the irony that after over fifty years treating animals as a veterinarian she had finally come to know a dog who could understand what she would say to him and now she could think of nothing to say.

The hour-long drive to Prometheacorp headquarters seemed interminable. As it was now evening the protestors outside the compound had thinned to only about one hundred individuals, and at the time Sally was escorted by the police through the gate they were not generally active, seated in groups around small fires, some involved with their handheld electronic devices. They barely noticed as she passed.

Inside the gate, she followed Sergeant Goodwin's vehicle around to the loading docks located at the rear of the facility. A small number of white-coated men which included Matheson were walking down the handicap ramp to meet them at the bottom.

Sally turned off her vehicle's engine and turned to look at Kane who had remained in the same position the entire trip.

"We'd better just get this over with, I guess," she said to him. "I wish I could go in your place."

Suddenly there was a loud rapping on her window. Irritated and startled, Sally swung open her door to find Matheson standing before her, extending his hand. She chose not to accept it.

"Our organization owes you a deep debt of gratitude, Ma'am," he said to her. "As a veterinarian, I'm sure you can appreciate the huge contribution animal research has made toward improving the lives of people throughout the world. The knowledge we'll gain in this particular instance will be of enormous value."

"A couple of billion dollars worth of value?" she asked. "Spare me. We're surrendering the dog unwillingly and at gunpoint."

Taken aback at her attitude, Matheson withdrew his hand. "Very well," he said turning to Sergeant Goodwin who was standing by his car. "Sergeant, please remove the canine from the vehicle."

The sergeant glanced at Sally then back at Matheson.

"Huh-uh," he said, shaking his head. "I'm not an animal control officer. My job was to escort this vehicle safely to your premises. That's all."

Matheson temper was rising. "Then instruct this woman to hand him over."

"Sir, you have a nice day now," Goodwin replied as he returned to his vehicle and drove away, followed by the second patrol car.

Rather awkwardly, Matheson turned to the other men behind him.

"Did you," he stammered, "did one of you bring a leash?"

One of the men rather reluctantly held forth a leash and muzzle. Matheson instructed him to remove the dog. Sally clenched her jaw as the man opened the rear door and leaned in, swiftly placing a muzzle over Kane's face.

"He doesn't need that," Sally said to the man. "This dog doesn't need a muzzle."

The man ignored her as he pulled Kane from the vehicle.

"You idiots!" she shouted. "This dog probably has more intelligence than all of you put together. Show some respect!"

"Intelligence does not necessarily guide emotions or temperament," Matheson replied. "This is merely a safety precaution. That's all. Now thank you and goodnight."

Matheson turned to join the others as they proceeded up the ramp, leading Kane behind them.

"That's the same as putting handcuffs on him!" Sally shouted after him. "Listen to me. He has more than simple intelligence. This dog has feelings and emotions and . . . ."

Without looking at her, Matheson raised a hand in a gesture of farewell as Kane trailed behind, head lowered and tail between his legs.

Sally knew that Kane must never have felt lonelier or more betrayed in his life than he felt at this moment. If she herself had ever felt worse, she couldn't remember when.

CHAPTER TWENTY-ONE

By morning the massive crowd outside the McLaughlin home had disbursed, feeling defeated and dismayed, betrayed by the very family they had vowed to protect. All that was left behind was litter and several handwritten signs mounted on fences and posts, some disparaging Prometheacorp and a few shaming the family for surrendering to the enemy. Now the protestors would take their fight to the door of the villains who held Kane captive. They vowed they would never abandon him.

Inside the home, Elizabeth and Sally had slept in while May, unable to sleep, lounged on a sofa in the den wearing her bathrobe. Ben's head rested in her lap, and she stroked his hair as she sipped coffee from a cup. She and Elizabeth had managed to get a sedative down him, and now he was breathing the heavy breath of sleep, occasionally twitching, still fighting even in slumber.

Elizabeth descended the stairs looking much the worse for wear having endured a pretty restless night herself. On the landing she yawned, taking in the sight on the sofa, then approached her mother and took her cup, offering a refill before disappearing into the kitchen. When she returned, she handed back the replenished cup and settled down by her feet at the far end of the sofa to drink from the cup she had gotten for herself.

After fortifying herself with a few sips of coffee, Elizabeth wondered aloud as she looked at Ben's sleeping form, "Mom, what are we going to do about him?"

May had no answer, but she knew what to expect in the days ahead. "He'll regress, I'm sure. Maybe he'll accept another dog in time, but I just don't know."

Elizabeth nodded. "Well, he'd probably expect the dog to measure up to . . . ." She was going to say Kane's name but couldn't bring herself to speak it, so strongly was she feeling the loss and now the tears began to flow as they had when she had cried herself to sleep. "There couldn't possibly be another like him."

The two of them sat in silence a while longer until Elizabeth finally asked, "Mom, what will they do to him in that place? Could they possibly . . . ?"

"Well," May replied, "there's no point in imagining what will happen to him. There's nothing we can do now. It's out of our hands. We just have to go on and try . . . try not to think about it."

But that was something both of them knew they couldn't do.

In the days that followed, Ben grew silent and sullen and regressed to a level even May had not foreseen. He became easily irritated, experienced high levels of anxiety, became hyperactive and acted out in ways that could not be controlled. The doctor who had treated Ben all his life for his disorder could offer little help other than to seek the consultation of other doctors and to express the hope that in time he would improve. The tone with which the doctor delivered his prognosis did not give May much optimism.

Tom Burch, seated behind his desk at Prometheacorp headquarters in consultation with Matheson and Elder, was growing weary of having to buoy the spirits of his employees.

The initial good cheer he first felt when Kane was finally within Prometheacorp confines was soon tested as he heard from a steady stream of underlings and board members who complained about the bad image the whole incident represented for the company and anyone affiliated with it.

"I'll assure you of this one last time," he said to Matheson and Elder (though he knew it would not be the last time he'd make that declaration), "no matter how much flak we take for acquiring the dog, once we've mapped the microchip and put it on the market, the income this corporation is going to realize will set new records. Those idiots can stand outside our gate and yell their damn fool heads off, but no one is going to shut us down. Eventually, the world will thank us, though begrudgingly, I expect."

"We're willing to be patient Tom, but the company could use a bit of cheering up just now," Elder counseled. "There's a lot of worry and anxiety, and that doesn't make for productive employees. And you can expect considerable ill feeling to be expressed by the shareholders at the annual meeting next week."

"Well, I don't know what they expect of me," Burch said, throwing his hands into the air. "Do they want me to give the dog back, throw away a billion dollars? They may say they're upset about the whole program but don't forget, our shares have been holding steady."

"Maybe . . . ." mused Elder, ". . . maybe we should face the issue head-on, put everyone at ease before they have a chance to voice a protest at the meeting."

"What do you propose?"

Elder wrinkled her brow in thought. "The main concern is the welfare of the dog."

"How are we treating the dog?" Burch asked Matheson.

The professor shrugged. "Well enough, I suppose," he said. "But . . . ."

Burch and Elder waited patiently for the rest of the sentence.

"Eventually," he continued, "we're going to have to perform surgery. We'll have to do some tests, disconnect and reconnect certain . . . ."

"What's that going to do?" Burch interrupted. "Could it kill the dog?"

Matheson shrugged again. "Perhaps. Or, it could cause permanent brain damage. We have no way of knowing until we start disassembling the whole thing to see how it operates."

Burch swore under his breath. "Keep this information quiet, you hear? We don't want that kind of information to get out right now. Those protestors out there will burn this place to the ground."

"You need to assure the shareholders that the dog is okay," Elder advised. "In fact, you need to *show* them he's okay."

"Is the dog okay right now?" Burch asked Matheson.

"Right now, yes," Burch replied, "but we need to proceed."

"Then that's what we'll do," Burch interrupted, standing up from his chair with enthusiasm. "We'll have the dog brought in to the shareholder's meeting. I've got a special way with dogs. We'll smother the damn canine with affection and dog cookies, and we'll convince them that we love this dog more than our own families. That's it!"

"But what will we do if the dog dies later when we perform the surgery?" Matheson asked.

"We tell them he died while we were performing *life-saving* surgery," Burch answered. "You can concoct some kind of disease the dog might have had, can't you? In fact, we let it leak out that even if the dog stayed with the kid, he was going to die of dog's disease, I don't know, whatever you want to call it. Our top animal doctors here found out he'd been sick for a long time, and they tried desperately, *desperately* to save him, but they were just too late. Just too damn late. We at Prometheacorp are devastated that this noble creature we loved so much was just too far gone, but we can be grateful that he left the gift of superior knowledge to mankind, who will be forever in his debt."

Burch stood smiling, his arms folded. He was tremendously pleased with himself.

Elsewhere, an armed guard was stationed in front of a heavy metal door in the laboratory building located nearby on the Prometheacorp campus. Behind the door in a cold, sanitized dog run painted an antiseptic white, Kane lay on a small bed that had been placed in the middle of the floor. A few rubber dog toys left untouched were scattered about the room and a silver bowl full of crystal clear water was stationed in one corner. He was never taken outside the laboratory so in another corner lay a sizeable section of artificial grass on which he was expected to relieve himself as the need arose. The entire scene was monitored by two video cameras mounted above and looming over the room was a large window behind which two lab technicians were stationed to observe the dog twenty-four hours a day and to make sure that the air in his pen was maintained at a constant temperature. A staff veterinarian inspected him daily to ensure his good health, but concern was growing over the dog's lack of appetite. A strict rule was in place forbidding any employee from getting close emotionally to the dog in order to maintain his position as a subject for study and research. When the time came for experimentation, the directors of the project wanted no sentimentality to interfere with whatever the laboratory technicians might be required to do.

For Kane, it was all clinically perfect and emotionally vacuous. There was no affection and no love, he was lonely and empty, and his heart was broken. He tried not to think of Sam or of Ben because it was too painful, but they were all he could think about and when he dreamed he dreamed of them.

CHAPTER TWENTY-TWO

In an effort to influence attendees, the Prometheacorp management team spared little expense in preparing for their Annual Shareholders Meeting. An event that might otherwise have been held in a large auditorium was this year presented in the largest convention hall in the grandest, most luxurious hotel in San Francisco. The newly built Hamilton-Walters Hotel was located within a short walk to Fisherman's Wharf and offered amenities few others could match, including a superlative lunch of various meats, fish and salads served to all who attended just prior to the start of the meeting.

The extravagance given to the shareholders, it had been emphasized, was not paid for with corporate funds. Tom Burch himself footed the bill. It was his way of proclaiming to his shareholders the optimism he held for the outcome of the Mastermind program. Though many in attendance were impressed with the luncheon presentation, a few pointed out that with the salary and benefits Burch was receiving the expense likely amounted to mere pocket change for the corporate CEO.

The shareholders felt that the elaborate lunch was the least they were due after having braved the throngs of protestors who jammed the street in front of the hotel, brandishing signs and yelling epithets at anyone who presented an official invitation to the dark-suited staff at the hotel door. Police were in heavy attendance, and a large squad of heavily armored riot police stood at the ready a mere block away.

The news media were well represented both outside the hotel and inside the meeting room, and there was heavy speculation among them that hostility from the shareholders toward Burch was expected to be on the menu following coffee and dessert. Fortunately for him, the anticipated success of the Burch miracle (as some were calling it), kept stock value fairly constant with no significant change. Burch knew that he needed to bolster confidence and convince the shareholders to hold tight.

High above the gathering, on the roof above the 34th floor, the large Prometheacorp executive helicopter touched down allowing Tom Burch and several associates to disembark. From the rear of the aircraft, two dark-suited guards accompanied a stainless steel crate large enough to hold a full-grown collie as it was unloaded and wheeled onto the roof by a serious looking man in a spotless white jumpsuit who guided the metallic object to the service elevator.

In a matter of minutes the elevator reached the first floor and as the doors opened the two guards proceeded down a service hallway followed close behind by the jump-suited attendant pushing the container.

As the authoritative looking party rounded a corner of the hallway, they were met by Luis, a young employee who was hastening from the opposite direction bearing an armful of soiled tablecloths on his way to the hotel laundry. One of the guards brusquely ordered him to step aside which Luis was able to accomplish only after some difficulty due to the narrowness of the passageway through which they were traveling. As the metal crate passed closely by him his curiosity was piqued by what appeared to be some kind of animal whose fur, sable, and white, he could barely make out through several air holes on the side of the container. As he stood for a moment watching it pass he could discern a brown eye peeking at him through one of the holes in the back as the crate continued on its trip down the hall. The expression in the eye gave him the impression that the creature inside was appealing to him for help. He observed the curious object inside which continued to watch him as the distance between the two of them increased until it was wheeled down the hallway around another corner and out of sight.

In due course, the two guards escorted the crate and accompanying attendant out of the service hall into one of the main arteries of the hotel where another guard signaled them through a doorway he opened. The entryway delivered them to a large room located next door to the meeting hall in which the shareholders were dining. Inside the room, a tall, thin woman sat reading a book as she waited for them to arrive. Next to her stood a spotless dog grooming table around which various metal boxes were arranged, their drawers open revealing numerous brushes, combs, hair sprays and even makeup, all tools of the type used by professional dog groomers when preparing for dog shows.

As the crate was rolled to a stop next to the table, the groomer placed her book aside and began preparing her tools while the attendant opened a door on the metal enclosure and lifted Kane from within and placed him on the counter. The guards pulled up chairs nearby and sat watching the groomer's actions with unconcealed boredom. The attendant secured the collie to the table grooming arm with a loop around his neck and then stood idly by as the groomer began briskly brushing Kane's dense coat. The dog stood in place, disinterested and aloof.

A door from an adjacent room opened wide, and Tom Burch swept in closely followed by Wyndham, Elder, and a hefty bodyguard. At the sight of their boss, the two guards accompanying Kane quickly stood at attention and simulated a look of interest in the groomer's activities.

Burch stopped grandly before the grooming table and nodded his approval.

"Fine. Fine," he said with a smile. Kane looked straight ahead.

"Now, remember our plan," Burch said addressing the attendant. "When I give you the signal you be ready to enter through the side door over there. When you come in (and this is extremely important), when you bring him to me, we want him to appear eager to see me, understand? We want everyone watching us out there to think —er— to believe the dog and I are great friends. Am I clear on that point?"

"Absolutely," declared the attendant confidently. Reaching into the pocket of his jumpsuit he withdrew a small cellophane package which he handed to the executive. "In that case sir, may I recommend you keep this bag in your pocket. Just before you call the dog to you, rip off the top. It contains an extremely strong smelling bait that dogs simply can't resist. When he smells that I assure you, sir, he will be your very best friend."

Burch took the object from him and after a quick glance at it, thrust it into the side pocket of his coat, "Excellent! I shouldn't need it, though. I have a special way with dogs. They just take to me, somehow. Always have."

He stood awkwardly for a moment observing the groomer's work on the dog before giving Kane a pat on the head. The attendant thrust forward a hand as a gesture of caution.

"If I may suggest, sir," he said, "dogs are not generally fond of being petted on the head and muzzle. Perhaps if you stroke the fur on the side of his neck instead, or maybe scratch behind one of his ears. If you do that, he'll be far more likely to appreciate your attention."

"Oh, I suppose that's true for some dogs," Burch responded dismissively, "but right now this fella and I are bonding. See?"

As if to confirm his claim, Kane licked his hand.

"Oh, yeah," Burch said with a chuckle. "Dogs have a special thing for me."

Elder pulled a small lint brush from her purse and swept away several strands of Kane's fur that had attached themselves to the lapel of his dark blue jacket.

"Okay," Burch said turning to Elder and Matheson, "Let's go over the report once more before it's time for me to go in." He led them to a table in a corner of the room, and Wyndham opened a briefcase he had been carrying and withdrew several sheets of paper which he spread out before them as they sat.

No one noticed that Kane, from his position on the grooming table, was watching Burch, studying him intently.

Inside the next room, the dining plates were being removed, and coffee was being served by the hotel staff as the guests talked among themselves and reviewed the slick looking annual report they had been given when they entered. No one seemed to be paying much attention to the Prometheacorp staff member who was delivering a rambling, welcome speech from the podium situated between two lengthy tables at the center of a slightly elevated dais at the front of the room where the board members were seated. Recognizing the various organizers of the event, his thanks were met with faint, indifferent applause from those few scattered about the room which seemed to be paying attention.

"Well," announced the speaker at length after attempting a poorly delivered joke that fell with a discernable thud, "I guess I've taken enough of your time so now comes the moment I'm sure everyone has been waiting for."

The side door opened, admitting Elder and Matheson who found seats behind the tables at the dais as the lights in the room began to dim and the crowd gradually fell to a hushed silence.

"Ladies and gentlemen," the speaker intoned with great importance, "it is with great honor that I introduce to you the Chief Executive Officer of our organization, Mister Prometheacorp himself, Thomas Burch!"

The lights in the room having completely dimmed, the speaker's podium was now brightly illuminated as the side door opened once again, and Burch strode swiftly to the front of the gathering, a business-like smile on his face, polite but not too broad as he raised a hand in greeting to the crowd which welcomed him with applause, uncertain and restrained. His bodyguard stationed himself at the door, surveying the audience carefully.

Arriving at a position just in front of the podium he raised his hand humbly to silence the applause, but he needn't have. The ovation had already ceased. At least no one booed, he thought to himself.

Choosing to address the crowd from in front of, rather than behind the podium, he started to speak before Elder promptly rose, grabbed a portable microphone and handed it to him.

Thanking her, Burch addressed his audience whose rapt attention he now held.

"Ladies and gentlemen, my fellow shareholders and members of the news media here today," he began, "regardless of all you have heard and read in the days leading up to this event, and despite the prophesies of doom and despair which those who disapprove of progress may have proclaimed, I am here this afternoon to declare to you that Prometheacorp Technologies today is healthy and profitable and that we now stand on the very brink of introducing to the world the most miraculous, exciting and, yes, profitable development in the entire history of the human race. Each and every one of you who have stood behind us with your investment dollars will, in just a few months, experience wealth beyond your wildest dreams. For your faith and confidence in this great organization and in the American dream that has made it all possible, the entire world will soon bestow on you, the shareholders of Prometheacorp, fervent and profound gratitude.

"We are indebted to the dedicated scientists and researchers employed by our organization, who are, without argument the most brilliant minds in the world today."

"Oh," he said suddenly breaking the solemnity of his address with a chuckle, "there is one more to whom we are indebted. You've all heard about this fella in the past few weeks, and I think it's about time you met him in person. Ladies and gentleman, I give you Kane, the smartest dog in the world!"

The side door swung wide, and Kane rushed in, wagging his tail and eagerly pulling at the end of the leash held by the attendant who trailed behind attempting to maintain control as the dog rushed toward Burch.

While the crowd gasped with surprise at the sight of the celebrity collie, Burch quickly opened the top of the bait bag he had been given and held it in his hand, releasing a strong and pungent smell of liver. After the attendees recovered from the surprise of seeing Kane, they burst into wild, uninhibited applause while smartphone cameras snapped away, flashing with the frequency one would see at a presidential press conference.

When Kane reached the executive, he energetically jumped up on him with his front paws, licking Burch's face enthusiastically. The attendant attempted to gain control of the dog, and with much effort finally managed to pull him off. Burch, laughing merrily, started to kneel down next to Kane but, finding that difficult, he gestured to the table, yelling over the adulation of the crowd to the dog handler to place Kane there. The attendant, complying with the order, awkwardly lifted Kane to the tabletop, knocking off a cup of coffee while the board members seated at that spot backed their chairs away from the table. The dog danced about, happily wagging his tail as he seemed to smile at the CEO.

Burch turned back to the audience to modestly accept their approval, and behind him, from the table, Kane leaned close enough to lick his ear, which caused him to giggle. The dog handler attempted to pull Kane back, but in so doing many in the crowd voiced their displeasure. Quickly realizing that the handler was dampening the effect, he was trying to get across, Burch, without warning, pulled the collar and leash from over

Kane's head and thrust them into the man's hands, gesturing for him to go wait by the door. The attendant started to object that this might not be a wise idea.

"Don't worry," Burch yelled into his ear as he shoved him off stage. "You'll see. Dogs have a special thing for me!"

Turning back to the audience who cheered even louder now that Kane was unleashed, Burch placed a hand on the dog and turned to pose for photos. After a lengthy interval, he raised his hand to quiet the crowd and picked up the microphone as he stepped forward to speak again.

"Folks," he said when the din had finally subsided, "in case any of you are still in doubt, I want to give you my solemn oath that no harm will ever come to this dog and let me assure you, he has never been happier in his entire life!"

He was suddenly interrupted by Kane, who barked in friendly agreement behind him.

Turning to the dog, Burch set the microphone down again and began vigorously patting Kane on the head, causing him to blink in reaction to the blows he was receiving.

Now was the time Kane had been waiting for, and it marked the end of the act he had thus far carried off so successfully.

At first Burch didn't hear the low growl that began to form in Kane's throat but gradually, as the sound increased in volume and ferocity, and as Kane's lip curled into an angry snarl, Burch's laughter caught in his throat, and as he recognized the sudden animosity that now revealed itself in the dog's eyes, he felt a sense of terror he had never before experienced.

The action that followed occurred rapidly. So fast in fact, that those who witnessed it were still applauding and laughing merrily at the activity that had taken place a scant few seconds before Kane abruptly altered his temperament.

From his position on the table, Kane could see one of the two main entryway doors at the back of the room being opened to admit a table bearing a large, spectacularly decorated cake. Recognizing his opportunity, he hastily seized it, loudly snarling at Burch who clumsily backed away. Free of the collar and leash that had so generously been removed, Kane gathered himself and launched from the table with great strength. His front paws pushed Burch backward, sending the man sprawling on his back on the floor before the stunned crowd, leaving the dog standing on his chest with all four paws, growling into his face. For a brief instant man and dog were thus engaged until Kane observed the package of liver snacks that had fallen next to Burch's neck. Quickly grabbing the package with his mouth, Kane shook his head angrily, sending the contents of the bag scattering and bouncing about the floor before dropping it, dripping with canine saliva, onto Burch's terrified face.

Screams were heard throughout the room as the crowd began to comprehend what was happening and began reacting in shock. Many sitting at the dais table stood quickly, sending china and glassware scattering. The bodyguard standing at the side door reached into his pocket and withdrew an oversized pistol, clutching the handle with both hands as he prepared to aim it at the dog. Elder, sitting near the guard, grabbed his arm.

"You stupid idiot! Put that way!" she screamed. "That dog is worth more than he is!"

The handler was falling over himself as he rushed, leash in hand, toward the dog but long before he came near, Kane pushed himself off Burch's chest and raced with lightning speed down a narrow passageway between the dining tables toward the open door. Several people attempted to catch him, grabbing at his fur and legs as he passed, but he was moving much too fast for anyone to manage a firm grip. One young man started whistling and vainly calling for Kane to "come" only to receive an incredulous look from a woman standing next to him. Near the back of the room, with the doorway almost within reach, a large man managed to tackle the dog momentarily, but before he could tighten his grasp, Kane managed to wriggle free and with mounting speed propelled himself onto the table that was being wheeled through the narrow opening of the door. Though he slipped on the icing of the cake which sat in the middle of the table, Kane was able to maintain his balance and in a flash jumped to the floor on the opposite end and darted away.

As it happened, Luis, the busboy who had encountered Kane as he had been carted into the facility earlier, was the individual now attempting to push the table which now stood in the doorway blocking all entrance and exit from the dining room. Though the entryway was a double door affair, the second door was now wedged against the table as a crowd of guards and other officials jammed against one another, yelling and pushing in an attempt to chase the dog.

If one looked very closely at Luis' face amid the hubbub, one might have discerned a very slight, if mischievous smile as he watched Kane race down the hall toward the entrance to the hotel lobby. Turning back to the crowd, who were now screaming obscenities as they attempted to push past the table blocking the doorway, Luis shouted at them in Spanish as he tried to clear the way, somehow only managing to wedge the table in more tightly. A hotel manager finally arrived on the scene, yelling at Luis to return to the kitchen as he took charge with the help of other members of the serving staff. Their efforts were of only minimal help.

Rounding a corner, Kane spotted an opening which appeared to lead to the main lobby, and he charged in that direction, maneuvering through the hotel guests who were mingling throughout. Several reacted with amusement as he rushed past them. He came to a sudden stop before the large glass doors that had all been closed securely against the assembled mass of protestors gathered on the sidewalk outside. A phalanx of police and hotel security were lined up inside the doors facing the crowd while another line guarded the doors from outside. None of the defenders noticed the collie that had entered the lobby, their attention having been directed toward those outside.

Kane turned with a sudden twist and raced across the room toward the entrance to one of the hotel's fine dining rooms. The host standing at the podium near the entrance failed to notice the dog as he rushed in, occupied as he was with a trio of guests who were checking their reservations. The rest of the waiting staff was similarly distracted with the distribution and consumption of food and beverages, and few patrons noticed the collie dog in the dimly lit room as he rushed by them heading for the kitchen. One patron who did notice laughingly told his waiter that the steak he had been served was so bad it should be given to the dog. The waiter failed to get the joke.

Elsewhere within the hotel, the doorway to the convention dining room had been cleared, and security and staff poured from the room in many directions in pursuit of the collie that had recently disrupted the annual shareholders meeting. At the front of the room, Burch had been helped to his feet and into a chair as underlings expressed their amazement and attempted to comfort him. Elder handed him a glass of water.

"We've got to catch that dog!" he exclaimed between gulps of water.

"We'll catch him, sir," a security guard assured him. "He can't get out of this hotel. Not with all of the security we have in place. The police will be here any minute."

"This is disaster," Burch gasped. Suddenly pulling himself up, he attempted to regain control. Turning to Elder, he commanded, "Get the word out. A reward! A two hundred thousand dollar reward to anyone who returns that dog to us unharmed. Got that?"

Nodding, Elder pulled out her cellphone and issued instructions.

A television news reporter stood nearby with a cameraman who had captured the CEO's order, and she motioned for the cameraman to follow her to the back of the room where a live broadcast was in progress. Speaking into the microphone as she faced the camera, she was the first to announce Burch's reward offer to the world.

Within the protest group outside the hotel, a young girl was checking her social media contacts on her phone when suddenly she screamed out to several who were gathered around her.

"Listen! Listen to this!" she cried. "Kane was here! He was here at the meeting inside!"

A larger group gathered around her and moved in close to hear what she had to say.

"He was here?" some of them asked incredulously. "Right here in front of us?"

"They must have snuck him in on a helicopter up on the roof or something," the girl figured.

"Hey, listen to this!" a young bearded man standing nearby shouted, holding his phone over his head. "He's gotten away from them. He's running around loose somewhere inside the hotel, and there's a reward! A *two hundred thousand dollar reward* to whoever returns him."

"Oh my god!" the girl yelled. "Everybody is going to try to get him now. We've got to get to him first and rescue him! We've got to find him before anybody else does!"

The news of Kane's escape inside the hotel and a plan to capture him was formulated and spread swiftly among everyone present as the crowd now grew louder and more menacing.

At that moment a large, dark, SUV escorted by several police vehicles, emergency lights flashing, pulled up between the protestors and the front doors of the hotel and a tall, dark police official who many in the crowd recognized as Jim Keaton, San Francisco Chief of Police, was escorted past the security barriers through the entrance to the hotel.

Beyond the excitement that had spread throughout the hotel, in a quiet storeroom near the kitchen, Luis was sorting and stocking various table linens as he stacked them on rows of shelving that lined the walls. It was one part of his job he didn't mind because of the silence the room afforded and because no one was snapping their fingers or barking at him. He relished the opportunity to work independently.

It must have been coincidence that as he reflected on the peculiar expression in the eye of the caged creature he had encountered earlier in the service hallway, he became aware of a heavy panting sound and he realized he was not alone in the room. Standing very still, his eyes searched for the source of the sound, and his gaze eventually settled on a laundry cart loaded with used linens that had been parked in a corner of the room. Slowly kneeling down and lowering his head close to the ground he squinted his eyes until his vision allowed him to see the area underneath and in that position he was able to distinguish the beautiful collie that lay behind the cart, panting heavily, his head resting between his paws. Luis quickly recognized that this was the same animal that had escaped the shareholders meeting and he smiled in recognition.

"Hey!" Luis said to the dog quietly. "What are you doing back there, my friend? Come out here and see me. Come on!"

At first reluctant, Kane concluded that this was someone he could trust and he cautiously stepped away from his hiding place to face Luis who seated himself on the floor and began scratching the dog behind the ear.

"Say, I know you!" Luis said to the dog. "You're that special dog, eh? The real smart one? You're the one they took away from that little boy so that big company can use you to make lots of money, right?" He struggled to remember the dog's name. "Uh, Kane, right? Is that you?"

Kane placed a paw in the man's lap.

"I'll bet those guys don't know you snuck in here, huh?" Luis continued. "You want to go back to the little boy? Is that where you're going? 'Lassie go home,' huh?"

The expression on Kane's face seemed to confirm Luis' deductions.

"You probably don't like those guys too much, do you?" he asked. "I don't blame you. I got a boy back home in Mexico. I love him very much, but I haven't seen him for a very long time. I wish I could be with him right now, just like you want to be with your friend."

As Luis' thoughts reflected on the son he left behind, he came to realize what he must do. Giving Kane a pat, he stood and approached the door and opened it just wide enough to see into the kitchen beyond. He could see the various staff hustling about preparing and delivering the food. Glancing over his shoulder toward Kane, he placed a finger to his lips and motioned toward him to stay where he was, then he cautiously opened the door just enough to slip through.

Within two steps of the door stood a serving cart stocked with beverages that had been loaded by one of the servers who now occupied himself with getting ice from a large machine nearby. Quickly grabbing two bottles of beer nestled among the other beverages, Luis retreated back to the linen room, pausing just long enough to ensure that he had not been observed before exiting and quietly closing the door behind him.

Kane watched with curiosity as his new friend rushed toward him, giggling and brandishing the two beers.

"No, no," Luis laughed, "these aren't for us. I don't think this stuff is supposed to be good for collies. Give you a headache, man!" He motioned for Kane to follow him and walked toward a large door at the opposite end of the room marked "EXIT." Pulling the door open just enough to peer outside, he squinted through the opening into the bright afternoon sunlight.

As he had expected, just beyond the loading dock that backed up to the door Luis spotted two uniformed guards leaning against a security patrol car parked several feet away. He could hear the two of them conversing as they played a video game on their cell phones, heedless of the turmoil building inside the structure they were charged with guarding.

"Ah! Perfect!" Luis said as he turned back into the room and knelt before Kane. "Now listen, I hear you're supposed to be a very smart dog, so you pay careful attention to what I have to say, OK? I'm going to go back out there and get those guys' attention. Got that? But I'm going to leave this door open a little bit, eh? So you watch me closely. When I motion to you, you come running, only go behind their backs, so they don't see you getting away, OK? Can you do that?"

Kane barked very softly.

"Good boy!" Luis laughed, roughing up the fur on Kane's neck.

Standing, he looked one more time through the opening in the door but then suddenly stopped and turned, looking at Kane. After looking into the dog's eyes, he quickly knelt and wrapped his arms around his neck, placing his face next to Kane's with a loving hug.

"You be very careful, my friend," Luis told him, his voice choking, "and when you get back to that little boy you don't ever let them take you away from him again, promise?"

Kane gently licked his new friend on the cheek.

From the kitchen, there arose a sudden swell of noise as several male voices began shouting questions at the kitchen employees.

"They're coming after you!" Luis declared, swiftly rising and wiping a tear from his eye. "Here we go. Watch me!"

Luis tucked the beer bottles under his arm and exited the back door, leaving it slightly ajar. Moving to the exit, Kane nudged the door open just far enough to let him view Luis' actions. From his position, he could observe his friend as he walked swiftly down a ramp and approached the two guards with a cheerful greeting. The salutation they returned left no doubt that they knew Luis and he was a welcome acquaintance. After a few quiet words were exchanged between the three men, Luis stealthily looked about before inviting them to join him in a crouch beside the car. Kneeling down with him, they were each handed a bottle of beer which they accepted eagerly and gratefully.

The noise in the kitchen was growing increasingly louder, and Kane became aware of footsteps moving ever closer to the door across the room from the exit. Focusing his attention on Luis, Kane waited for the signal to move and when it finally came, unseen by the two guards, Kane rushed through the door, pausing just long enough on the other side to nudge it closed but leaving it open just enough to allow Luis re-entry when needed.

Luis' plan worked perfectly as Kane, undetected, scurried down the ramp and raced past the security vehicle, turning into the alley that ran behind the hotel. He paused only long enough to convey to Luis his thanks with a grateful look and a bow.

Unnoticed by the guards, Luis waved a goodbye to his friend and Kane was gone.

CHAPTER TWENTY-THREE

Chief Keaton, accompanied by several officers, made his way to the shareholders' luncheon room as he brushed past the steady stream of shareholders who had been instructed by Elder to leave the hotel in order that a search could be mounted to find Kane. Though some complied, many continued to slink through the halls, opening doors and peeking beneath tables in the hope that they would be lucky enough to find the dog. Instead, most were apprehended by hotel staff and escorted from the premises.

Inside the luncheon room, the police chief found that some of the shareholders stubbornly remained at their tables. Burch, surrounded by concerned executives, was seated in a chair near the podium wiping the sweat from his face with a cloth napkin while staffers attempted to remove the various media reporters and cameramen that were jockeying for a position near him.

Nodding toward the reporters, Keaton ordered two of his officers to lend a hand to the Prometheacorp employees, and two of his men scrambled to comply. As he marched toward the podium, he was hailed with some relief by Burch.

"Jim!" Burch greeted him. "Thank God you're here! I'm going to owe you one for this."

"I'll put it on your tab," the police chief responded. "Am I to understand you've called the head of the San Francisco Police Department down here to help you find a missing dog?"

"It's more than just a missing dog," Burch said, hurt at the annoyance in Keaton's voice. "You know that. This is the most valuable creature on the face of the earth."

Keaton removed his hat and scratched his head as he seated himself. "Well, I don't know. Missing dogs are the jurisdiction of the San Francisco Animal Care and Control unless he was stolen."

"Dammit, Jim," Burch angrily exclaimed. "You know the situation here. Now, what can you do to help me?"

"Right now I'm helping you by keeping that mob outside from ripping your throat open. We'll put out an APB to be on the lookout, but I'm afraid I can't spare any personnel to go combing the streets of San Francisco looking for a lost dog. I hear you've offered a sizeable reward. That's the best anyone can do right now."

"You're on their side, aren't you?" Burch said nodding toward the front of the hotel. "You want that dog to go back to the kid. You don't care about all the money my company could lose over this."

Keaton stared at Burch for a moment, a look of disappointment covering his face. Finally, he rose from his seat, placing his hat back on his head.

"All right, Tom," he said, "here's what I can offer you. We have an outside organization that assists us with bloodhounds when we're searching for a missing person. The dogs will be here in a few minutes and odds are pretty good they'll find this collie of yours. Good luck."

With that, Keaton turned on his heel and marched from the room followed by his company of officers. Barely out of earshot, he was heard to mutter under his breath, "But I hope they don't."

Kane proceeded cautiously but swiftly as he left the vicinity of the hotel. He had narrowly escaped a frenzied crowd that had found their way to the rear of the building, causing the two security guards to choke on their beers as they jumped to their feet. The crowd rushed toward the receiving dock and were met by the hotel staff who had just passed through the exit door that they found slightly ajar. Kane observed with satisfaction as all participants, staff, protestors, and security, engaged in noisy, animated argument.

Another group of individuals raced around to the back of the hotel, and it became impossible to discern who was searching for Kane for the purpose of rescue and who was searching in order to collect the reward. It didn't matter, really. Everyone was looking for him.

Hiding temporarily within shrubbery not far from the hotel, Kane had little time to determine his eventual destination. He knew that humans lacked the gift of scent bestowed on canines, but he couldn't be sure that they wouldn't soon locate him. He had to put distance between himself and his pursuers, and he knew he had to do it quickly. He would first find somewhere to hide, someplace where he could plan his next move.

Kane cautiously slipped from the greenery where he had been concealed and found himself on a sidewalk that passed through a busy commercial area. Heavy foot traffic and vehicle gridlock on the streets caused him to realize this was not the best place to remain unseen.

He quickly adopted one trick that he figured might work for a while at least. Spotting a young, nicely dressed woman who was deeply involved in a phone conversation, he rushed to her side and walked at her pace, making it appear that he was with her and that they were simply out for a late afternoon walk. He could only hope that no one would notice that she was walking her dog off leash. As she walked, her sight was directed toward the various merchant window displays she passed which she looked at but didn't really see as her attention was really focused on her phone discussion. Kane was careful to stop at the street corners when she stopped, and he resumed walking the moment she did the same. He restrained himself from the urge to greet other dogs he met on the way.

Along the sidewalk, Kane did not go unnoticed as several passers-by remarked on the wonderful collie and how obedient he was to walk at his mistresses' side off leash.

"Beautiful! Beautiful!" commented one lady in passing.

"Thank you," Kane's adopted owner responded vainly as she primped her hair and continued talking on the phone, not realizing the remark referred to the dog at her side.

With great difficulty, Kane maintained his steady pace as a policeman on a motorcycle wound his way through the stalled traffic, his siren blaring. The dog was able to relax somewhat when the policeman continued past.

The ruse finally came to an end in an area where the traffic on the street began to move, and the lady stopped to hail a passing taxi. As a yellow cab pulled to the curb, the woman concluded her phone conversation and reached for the door.

Calling across to her from his position behind the steering wheel, the driver yelled out to her, "Sorry, ma'am. No dogs," and swiftly pulled back into traffic.

"What?" the woman called after him, completely bewildered. Looking about her, she saw no dog. Kane had already placed a considerable distance between the two of them.

Assuming the cab driver had just insulted her, she yelled an angry expletive in his direction.

Kane watched from behind a trash can sitting nearby as she stomped her foot and continued down the sidewalk, attempting to hail another cab. Looking about, he took stock of his surroundings and considered his options. At that moment a sound from the distance reached his ears, and he tilted his head slightly to hear it more clearly. Before he was able to identify the source of the sound his nose told him exactly what was headed in his direction.

Bloodhounds. Several of them. He had not overestimated his pursuers' ability to find a way to locate him, and from the occasional distinctive bloodhound howl, he knew they were on his heels and would soon be facing him. Wasting no time, Kane propelled himself among the numerous pedestrians crowding the sidewalk, weaving in and out with little regard for the fact that some nearly fell down to avoid colliding with him.

Crossing into traffic at each street corner he ignored signals as cars swerved to avoid hitting him and horns were sounded. Fortunately, the traffic was moving slowly, minimizing the danger.

The attention he was drawing to himself placed his freedom at great risk, but he knew he had to outdistance the hounds that were drawing nearer with every second. Turning into an alleyway, he rushed past a large flatbed delivery truck parked at the rear entrance to a small market located on the bottom floor of one of the apartment buildings. For a moment, Kane contemplated jumping onto the flatbed in the hope that it would transport him from the scene and out of reach of the bloodhounds, but he quickly abandoned the idea. The driver of the truck was inside the market settling his delivery bill with the manager, and there was no way to know how soon he would return. Added to that was the slow speed of traffic. Kane's pursuers would likely catch up to him within a block or two.

He rushed around the truck and continued down the alley but was soon stopped short by an enormous brick wall. The alley was a dead end. There was no choice but to retrace his steps and continue his flight down the busy sidewalk. Hastening past the truck again, Kane stopped at the alley entrance and cautiously peeked around the corner in the direction from which he had fled. The sound of the bloodhounds had stopped momentarily as they attempted to recapture the scent they had briefly lost. From Kane's position, he could see them less than two blocks away as they recovered his trail and eagerly renewed the hunt.

Kane figured that he was not likely to outrun them for long. Desperately looking back into the alley from which he had just emerged, the truck caught his attention again, but this time it gave him new inspiration. Barely within leaping distance just above the cab of the truck, he spotted the second story landing of a metal fire escape which clung to the side of the apartment building in which the market was located. Kane wasted no time considering the odds of his ability to make the leap to the metal structure. The window of opportunity narrowed as the driver of the truck stepped into the cab and started the engine, and the hounds grew closer.

With uncanny strength and speed, the great collie rushed to the flatbed of the truck at the exact moment the driver began backing his way out of the alley. A leap from the bed to the top of the truck cabin and from there a larger, near impossible leap to the escape landing from which the truck was now distancing itself resulted in a near miss, but the jump miraculously came close enough to enable Kane to reach the top of the railing around which he wrapped his forepaws tightly. Another burst of strength would be necessary to boost him over the top as his front paws began to slip, threatening to send him backward onto the pavement below. There was nothing to it but to give it his greatest effort.

Somehow, at that instant, an image crossed his mind. It was the image of the boy he loved, and that vision triggered the force within him he needed to pull himself up and over the rail. Falling hard upon the grated floor of the landing his energy was nearly gone but there was no time to rest. With every ounce of strength remaining, he began climbing the stairs up the sixteen flights that would eventually deliver him to the roof.

Below him, six bloodhounds led by their handlers reached the alley entrance. Though they at first passed the cutoff, they soon circled back as the beasts followed Kane's trail down the back street, reaching the dead end and circling back. But suddenly the trail vanished.

The hounds excitedly sniffed their way through nearly every inch of the pavement but continually stopped in one spot. Their handlers were confused by this behavior, and they grew angry, yelling at the dogs to continue, but their commands were useless. The hounds could not pick up a trail that didn't exist.

CHAPTER TWENTY-FOUR

Elizabeth answered the ringing phone at the McLaughlin home with a cautious, "Hello," hoping the caller was not another reporter asking about the news of Kane's escape.

"Elizabeth," said the voice at the other end, "this is John Hadley."

"Oh John," she replied wearily, "not you, too. We haven't had any updates and . . . ."

"Hold on," he interrupted. "I'm calling with an update for *you*. This is a conference call. I have Sally on the line with me."

Elizabeth heard Sally's voice say hello as Hadley continued. "Please get your mother on the line. We need to talk."

May had just entered the room, and Elizabeth told her to grab the extension in the kitchen. When May picked up the line, Hadley explained the reason for his call.

"I've had another contact with Old Yeller, my secret contact at Prometheacorp," began Hadley. "He's managed to persuade a friend of his to hand him some of the research papers pertaining to the work they're going to be doing on Kane, and I believe we may have some good news. Well, sort of."

May welcomed any semblance of good news, and she chided Hadley for his preamble, urging him to get to the point.

"Apparently," he continued, "there is a way to disable the microchip embedded in Kane without surgery. If we can manage to get him to you, Sally, do you have access to any kind of radiation equipment?"

"Well, yes," she responded. "If you can get him to my office at the clinic, but I won't know . . . ."

"No, no," Hadley interrupted. "Don't worry. I'm going to email documentation to you that Old Yeller acquired. With your veterinary expertise, I'm hoping you'll be able to figure out how to conduct the procedure. I've been assured it's relatively easy."

"All right," Sally said bravely. "Get me the documentation, and I'll see what I can do, but . . . ."

Elizabeth continued Sally's sentence. "You're talking about disabling the mechanism that controls Kane's advanced intelligence."

"Yes, I am," Hadley confirmed, "but don't you see? If we essentially destroy that mechanism and he reverts to his normal, average, canine intelligence, he'll be useless to Prometheacorp. There'll be no reason for them to keep him anymore. He can come home."

There was silence from all participants on the party line until Hadley continued. "Listen, Sally, check your email and study those documents. I have a team of people I can trust working with me to locate Kane. When we get him back, we'll figure out a way to get him to your clinic so you can perform the procedure. Hopefully, it works. I gotta go now. I'm in a rush. Talk to you soon!"

There was a click on the line as Hadley disconnected but those remaining lingered in silence.

"Well," Elizabeth said, "they've got to find him first. With that reward money out there the whole world is going to be looking for him. They're bound to get him before we do."

"There's something else to consider," Sally added. "It will change him. He won't be the same. I don't know if Ben will understand."

"We can't worry about that. Not now," May said putting the receiver back in its charger.

Many miles away, with his last remaining bit of strength, Kane painfully pulled himself onto the roof above the sixteenth floor of the apartment building whose fire escape he had just scaled. This accomplished, he lay upon the spot where he landed, panting heavily as he longed for water to quench his overwhelming thirst.

With tremendous effort, he eventually managed to pull himself to his feet and jump to the top of a wooden, square covering located in the middle of the roof that had been built to protect some of the building air conditioning equipment. That spot provided him a full view in all directions over the four-foot safety wall that encircled the roof, and from there the panorama of the entire city of San Francisco surrounded him. His attention focused on the bay and his options for crossing to the other side.

Above him, the sound of an approaching helicopter captured his attention, and at that same time a nearby door leading onto the roof swung open, and a plump, elderly lady emerged. Spotting Kane, she motioned for him to jump down from the wooden covering.

"Get down!" she called to him. "Get down! They'll see you for sure up there!"

Kane, at first poised to fly, recognized her attempt to help him and he jumped down and huddled close to the side of the wooden covering as she rushed to him, pulling a thin blanket from under her arm.

"Stay under here until they've passed," the lady instructed him as she spread the blanket, covering him completely. Having made certain he could not be seen, she walked casually to the wall and braced herself against it, shading her eyes from the setting sun as she watched the aircraft hover nearby. Smiling, she waved a friendly greeting toward the airborne craft which lingered a moment longer before banking and moving away as it appeared to search the area. The woman waited until she felt it was safe before returning to Kane and gently lifting the blanket from him.

"What a beauty you are," she exclaimed in a soft, tender voice that immediately put Kane at ease. "Why, you're even more beautiful than all the pictures they've been showing of you on TV."

Still huddled against the side of the wooden box, Kane managed to gently wag his tale in gratitude as he continued to pant heavily.

"I saw you outside my window as you were making your way up here," she explained to him. "I would have left you alone but I heard the helicopter, and I thought perhaps you could use a little help."

As Kane licked his lips, she gasped, "Oh my goodness, how inconsiderate of me. Water. You need some water, don't you? Well, you stay right where you are. I'll take care of that, and I'll be right back. Don't go away!"

With that, she hustled away with a noticeable limp and exited back into the doorway through which she had entered.

Kane stood and walked to the wall, lifting his front paws to lean against it, enabling him to see over. He sniffed the breeze that floated up from below, and he carefully studied the view of the bay beyond. Gazing across the body of water an idea occurred to him, and he began mentally devising a plan. He was still leaning against the wall when the lady returned with a bowl of water, a folding chair and a plump, grey striped cat tucked under her arm.

Kane rushed to greet her, and she hardly had time to set the water bowl down before he began lapping up the cool refreshment. The lady smiled and watched him drink before unfolding her chair. The cat under her arm observed the dog with curiosity but with no alarm.

"You're quite the celebrity," she remarked good-naturedly as she seated herself with some exertion. "If you're really as smart as they say you are, you'll understand what I'm saying."

Kane paused in his drinking, looked up at her and swiftly waved a paw in the air, signifying his understanding.

"Excellent!" the lady said with a gasp and a chuckle. She stroked the fur of the cat in her lap as he purred and kneaded his claws on her leg. "Well, I want you to know that you have nothing to fear as long as you're in my company. I know your whole story, and I would never turn you in for reward money. They couldn't pay me enough."

His thirst quenched, Kane wearily reclined in front of her, wagging his tail in gratitude.

"Oh," she said, suddenly remembering, "where are my manners? You can call me Martha and my roommate here is Jack. That's short for Jack the Ripper. He has a great talent for shredding the draperies and the furniture."

Jack jumped from her lap and after lightly smelling Kane's nose, began rubbing against him affectionately.

"He trusts you," the lady said. "I hope you'll trust me too. Now, what's your plans after your daring escape?"

Kane looked into her face with a blank expression. There was really no way to convey to her the plan he was formulating.

"I thought so," she continued. "No idea. Well, you can't go back to your home, I'm afraid. They would just have to return you to those big money guys, wouldn't they? No, we'll have to figure out something else. I'm not sure just what. You can hide out here with Jack and me, but that won't be practical for very long."

She watched him for several minutes, buried deep in thought.

"Tell you what. For now, let's just enjoy each other's company, what do you say? The sun is setting, and it's going to be nice and warm tonight. I'll go downstairs and see what I can put on the stove, and we'll share a dinner and just spend the evening together. Then tomorrow we'll wake up rested and refreshed and figure out what we're going to do. How does that sound?"

Jack playfully swiped at Kane's gently wagging tail, which was the only response Martha needed.

As the evening sky gave way to twilight and the city lights gradually dominated the darkness, Martha made several trips through the rooftop access, returning with food, blankets, and a camping lantern and together with Kane and Jack, spent a relaxing and cordial evening regaling them with stories of her youth. Though Kane found it difficult to remain awake, he remained attentive and courteous toward this special lady who provided him sanctuary, sustenance, and solace.

As the evening wore on, another idea occurred to her, and she struggled to her feet, instructing Kane and Jack to remain while she fetched a few items to make the evening complete. She returned minutes later with a small mattress, pillows and a guitar upon which signs of age and wear on every inch of its surface evidenced its special place in Martha's heart.

After putting together a makeshift bed which she spread out on the rooftop, she lowered herself onto the mattress and propped her back into a semi-reclining position using the pillows for support. As Jack joined her on one side, Martha invited the drowsy collie to join her on the other. He found just enough space on the mattress opposite the cat, and he luxuriated in the most comfort he had known since he was taken away from Ben. He never found comfort in the bedding that had been provided for him in the laboratory, and now he knew why. To be truly comfortable, one needs more than a soft bed.

Martha strummed and picked at the strings of her guitar for several minutes, searching for just the right song for the occasion before noticing Kane's sleepy, dark brown eyes.

"Ah," she said. "Here's the one."

She gently strummed an accompaniment as she sang to Kane and as she did so, the sound of the city and sirens below seemed to fade away. Her voice was, he decided, the sweetest, most precious, most comforting sound his ears had ever heard.

> *"Beautiful, beautiful brown eyes*
> *Beautiful, beautiful brown eyes*

Beautiful, beautiful brown eyes
I'll never love blue eyes again."

Those were the only lyrics Kane heard before he fell into a deep, satisfying sleep. Several hours later he woke suddenly, aware that the music stopped and he stood, examining Martha as she slept, her head resting back on her pillows, a light snore in her throat, her cat and beloved guitar at her side. With his mouth, the collie carefully pulled the blankets that lay in a heap at her feet up and over until her shoulders were covered. After assuring himself that she was safe and warm, he settled down again next to her and resumed his blissful sleep.

Even the rising sun, unencumbered with the filter of morning clouds and haze shining into Martha's face failed to wake her the next day. That responsibility was assumed by the two men who rushed through the rooftop access door at 7 AM. Though Martha was at first undisturbed, Jack immediately leaped to his feet, arching his back and hissing his disapproval at the sudden appearance of the intruders.

One of the men, who appeared to be in his forties and wearing a sweater, began to vigorously shake her shoulder, calling out loudly, "Mom! Mom! Wake up!"

After several attempts, Martha began to stir and laboriously brought herself up into a sitting position. After rubbing her face, she tried to focus her eyes on her son who now knelt beside her.

"Oh, it's you, Ronald," she said with a smile and a hug around the neck. "What brings you over so early?"

"You called me last night," her son reminded her. "Remember? You said the collie was here with you."

Martha thought for a moment before finally remembering the call she made during one of her trips into her apartment the night before.

"That's right," she said. "I told you I needed your help to hide Kane from . . . ." She stopped in mid-sentence and looked about the roof. "Where is Kane? Where did he get off to so early in the morning?"

While searching the roof for the dog, her eyes lighted on the man who accompanied her son.

"Who's this?" she asked.

"His name is John Hadley," Ronald replied. "It's okay. He's on our side. It took me all night to track him down. He has a plan to help Kane."

"Where is he?" Hadley asked frantically. "Are you sure he's here?"

"If my mother says he was here, she's telling the truth," Ronald snapped. "She's doesn't have dementia and . . . . OK, sometimes she likes to spend the night up here on the roof with her cat and guitar, but I assure you she's not crazy or anything like that."

"Oh he was here all right," Martha said, steadying herself on her son's arm as she pulled herself to her feet. "I guess he decided to strike out on his own. He probably didn't want to be a burden. That dear, sweet boy."

"Okay," Hadley said, suddenly taking charge. "Where would he go next? He won't go home. He'll go someplace he knows, where he thinks he'll be safe. But where?"

Standing with the palm of his hand across his forehead he tried to recall everything the McLaughlin family had told him about the dog. As he searched his memory the sound of a cell phone vibrating interrupted and he quickly pulled it from his pocket and answered as Martha and her son watched him.

"Where, exactly?" Hadley spoke to the caller. "Do you think? Okay, that makes sense, so standby. I'm going to scramble my volunteers, and I'll call you back with a plan."

Hadley tossed the phone back in his pocket and rushed to the retaining wall. His eyes scanned the length of the San Francisco Bay until finally, he focused on one particular object. He slammed his fist down on the wall with an exclamation.

"What?" asked Ronald.

"There's a mountain path near the home he used to live in with the old man," Hadley informed him. "Odds are, that's where he's headed. Across the bay."

"How do we know what path he'll take to get there?" Ronald wondered.

"I have a team of volunteers looking out for him, and they've already reported sightings," Hadley replied. "He's on the move, and he's headed to the most direct route across the bay."

Martha and her son looked in the direction Hadley was pointing. Not very far away, they could see, spanned the Golden Gate Bridge.

CHAPTER TWENTY-FIVE

Police Chief Keaton was about to bite into an over-filled breakfast burrito while his security entourage surrounded his vehicle which was parked at the curb nearby. His driver often made this stop at a downtown food truck at his request during his regular morning drive to headquarters, and this morning the Chief was hoping to enjoy his breakfast uninterrupted for a change. That was not to be.

A police cruiser pulled up behind his SUV, and a captain jumped out and greeted him.

"Sir, we've located the dog," the captain reported.

Looking longingly at his burrito, Keaton asked for a report.

"He's nearing the south entrance to the Golden Gate Bridge, sir," came the reply.

"Hmm," Keaton said, contemplating his options. "Okay, Captain Moreno, I want the bridge blocked in both directions to all traffic, including pedestrians. That way we'll have him hemmed in on both sides so he can't escape. Have our men follow him close behind but not too close. We don't want him to panic and cause a problem before we can catch him. Get ahold of animal control and tell them to be ready for him on the other side. Get a copter to watch him from the air. And don't forget, he has to be captured alive, and there is to be no tranquilizer gun. One slight miscalculation could wind up killing the dog. Understood?"

Captain Moreno acknowledged, then paused before asking, "You want us to seal off the bridge?"

"Affirmative," his superior confirmed. "We need to catch that damned dog, so this city can get back to normal and so I can at least eat a breakfast burrito in peace."

Nearing the Golden Gate Bridge soon after, Kane paused, concealed behind roadside shrubbery, in order to observe the activity taking place near the toll booth entries. The few remaining pedestrians on the east side walkway were being hurried off, and the gate was closed behind them. This limited Kane's access and he determined that his only alternative was to cross the bridge using the vehicle access. A squad of police cars sat in the lanes entering the bridge preventing autos from passing, and the last vehicles permitted to enter from the other side were filtering across.

Kane knew that the chances for his being able to cross the bridge without being captured were not good. He couldn't possibly outrun any vehicle that might choose to chase him, but he knew he could outrun anyone who might step out of a vehicle to try to grab him. He also had the advantage of maneuverability, which might enable him to dodge and feint his way through spots that couldn't be accessed by cars. The bridge had been cleared which allowed him a wide open crossing once he managed to get past the police at the toll booths, but it would require all of his energy to make the complete run across the bay, a distance of over one and one-half miles. As for what awaited him on the other side, he could only guess but his view from the rooftop the evening before told him there were plenty of places to hide when and if he made it across.

After considering his chances, Kane opted to go for it.

Stealthily moving from his concealment, he slinked slowly toward the bridge toll booths. Most of the police were outside of their cars conversing with one another. Captain Moreno was encircled by a large group of officers as he delivered instructions on how to handle the situation. Others remained in their cars, attention focused on their phones. No one was posted to watch for the dog.

Kane moved between the vehicles, slinking low, cautious and unnoticed. He was about to pass the police cars in the front position of the line when an officer stepped from one of them holding his phone high in the air, calling out to Moreno.

"Sir!" the officer shouted. "Somebody just tweeted that the dog is crossing the bridge!"

Moreno and everyone around him turned to look at the bridge that spread out behind the toll booths. They saw nothing. As they turned back, an officer in one of the lanes suddenly spotted Kane as he cleared the first line of vehicles and began trotting past the toll booths.

"Hey!" the officer shouted, and everyone saw the dog at the same time.

Now it was time for Kane to move and he immediately broke into a run as the police, caught off guard, scrambled to their vehicles in a disorganized body, starting their cars, lighting up their red lights and accelerating their engines.

The chase was officially on.

A lengthy queue of impatient traffic lined the highway behind the police, waiting for the re-opening of the bridge. Nearly three-quarters of a mile back stood John Hadley, leaning against his open passenger door, phone to his ear as he tried in vain to see the action taking place ahead at the bridge entrance.

"It looks like he's on his way to your side," Hadley said to someone on the other end of the phone line.

"Okay," replied a voice, breathing heavy. "I managed to get to the scenic lookout just in time. I think I've spied a way across, but it's not going to be easy, and even if I make it onto the bridge, Kane may not want to go with me. I wasn't his favorite person, and we didn't part on the best of terms, but I'll do the best I can to persuade him."

"Use your charm," Hadley responded. "Do your best to persuade him. Now, my team isn't far behind you, and they're ready to go. I'm going to signal them to get into place right now, and your double is in his spot so we should be set. Listen, Old Yeller, or whoever you really are, the information you've been feeding us these past few weeks has been invaluable, and the risk you're about to take is enormous, but you're a hero. You got that? A real hero."

"Well," said the other caller, "since this will likely cost me my job and get me a jail sentence, and if I'm going to be a hero, you may as well get my real name for the news article you're going to write. I'm Nick. Nick Stanley."

Before Hadley could respond, Nick abruptly disconnected the call. An animal control truck was pulling into place on the northbound side of the bridge while a half dozen police cars blocked access to all other vehicles.

"Huh-oh," Nick muttered to himself as he jumped into his car, revved his engine and peeled out through the entrance that led to the lookout where he had been stationed. The bridge southbound traffic lanes were not blocked on the lookout side giving him easy access as he headed onto the bridge traveling north in the southbound lanes while the police behind him shouted. As Nick began sweating profusely, he prayed he would not run into any oncoming traffic, and he pushed his car's accelerator to the floorboard hoping he would meet Kane, racing from the opposite direction before he was captured by the police.

In his position on the city side of the bridge, Hadley found an internet broadcast that was transmitting a video signal of Kane's pursuit from one of several news helicopters that hovered overhead. Hadley was not the only one watching. In fact, all local television programming had been preempted by the special report. Viewers were accustomed to watching car chases on TV before, but this chase was unique and everyone tuned in.

A friend had placed a call to Elizabeth who promptly turned on the television and called out to her mother. Ben was in the kitchen, idly playing with Legos on the dining table but his mother went rushing to the TV.

Kane was making his run across the bridge physically alone, and yet many were with him. In her apartment, Martha was laughing aloud as she watched the broadcast, stroking Jack the Ripper's fur and cheering Kane on. Sally, summoned to her television, felt her heart beating loudly as she watched. From a monitor in his office, Burch could barely contain himself, swearing because the police were merely following the dog in a low-speed chase. And from a television set up in the kitchen of the Hamilton-Walker Hotel, as elsewhere, all work came to a halt as the employees watched and cheered Kane's audacious dash from the City of San Francisco.

"*Prisa, mi amigo!*" Luis shouted joyfully. "*Prisa!*"

The wind traveled through Kane's thick fur as he found an energy deep within to carry him across the bridge while dozens of police vehicles, their red lights rotating frantically, followed a few feet behind, while police and television broadcast helicopters hovered overhead, and while reporters breathlessly communicated details of the pursuit.

Though it was the collective hope that the collie would make good his escape, there was little confidence that such a thing was possible given the armada massed against him. How could he escape from the all-seeing eye of the helicopters, the television viewers wondered? How could he outrun a foot pursuit while his energy waned as it seemed to be doing with every passing minute? All of this was remarked upon by the news commentators with an air of regret as television audiences shook their heads.

Halfway across the bridge, Kane's energy was running out. His only hope for escape was headed straight for him from the opposite direction, and it was one of the television news reporters who first noticed as the helicopter cameras focused on the wrong-way driver.

"Here he comes!" shouted a reporter into his microphone, "Look at that car go! He's driving at maximum speeds, traveling the wrong way and that driver appears to be headed toward this dog. What can his motive be? Is he trying to rescue him or maybe collect the reward or is he just doing this for attention? Well, we'll soon know because the driver is quickly narrowing that distance between him and the dog!"

"Oh boy! Oh boy!" Nick repeated to himself as his car raced forward. Never in his life had he ever attempted anything as daring or as rebellious and yet as he approached Kane and the oncoming mass of law enforcement he felt a strange tickle inside. Damned if he wasn't enjoying it!

Kane, his tongue hanging heavily from the side of his mouth, marked the auto speeding swiftly toward him. Confused, he wavered in his pace until the car began to reduce speed just prior to reaching him.

The police braked their vehicles and jumped out, drawing their weapons as they braced themselves behind the open doors of their cars, prepared, if necessary, for a standoff with the driver headed toward them.

Still moving fast, Nick slammed his foot on his brake pedal, sending him skidding in a circle around Kane and facing the direction from which he had just traveled, leaving the collie cowering in place, frightened and confused. Nick impressed himself with this particular stunt, never having attempted it before. Captain Moreno and several of his men meanwhile began running on foot toward Kane.

Reaching across the seat, Nick grabbed the door handle and pushed open the passenger door, allowing Kane entrance. The dog pulled back, declining the open invitation.

"Kane, get in!" Nick shouted. "I'm on your side. Listen, you've got to trust me. I'm the only chance you've got of getting out of here! Please! Come on! It's now or never!"

The dog was still hesitant. Looking toward the police, he saw the group running toward him on foot. They were closing in on him, and Kane knew he had no more strength to outrun them. He had no choice but to trust this previously untrustworthy acquaintance. With only a moment to spare, he jumped into the passenger's seat of the car and Nick once again pushed the accelerator pedal to the floor, sending one officer to the ground who was in mid-flight and about to tackle Kane. The sudden acceleration caused the passenger door to slam shut, and Kane attempted to gain his balance.

The police watched Nick's car race away as they yelled at him to halt, then turned and ran back to their vehicles. Jumping in, they turned on their sirens which screamed as they took off after the dognapper who had clutched their prize from out of their hands.

"Listen!" shouted Nick to Kane. "It's going to get a little bumpy ahead, so you're going to need to hang on. I can get you out of this, but you've got to do exactly as I say and you're going to have to move immediately when I tell you to. You got that?"

With no hands to hang on with, Kane lay down on the seat in a huddle, preparing for whatever lay ahead.

The dog had already run most of the distance across the bridge, so the remaining stretch to the other side was quickly covered while Nick nervously watched the police who were following at a moderate speed behind him. In pursuit cases such as this, their training taught them to maintain a distance behind the vehicle being pursued and to take no action unless public safety was at risk. In time, they knew, the fleeing vehicle would either run out of gas or the driver would surrender. With the police helicopter watching overhead, the suspect didn't stand a chance.

Soon Nick reached the terminus of the bridge. A couple of wooden saw-horse barricades had been placed across all lanes, but they were purely symbolic, and the hood of Nick's car sent them splintering in all directions as he crashed through them, speeding along the highway into the hills that dominated the area on that side of the bridge.

"Now," Nick said to Kane, "if everything goes according to plan, we should be reaching the point of our escape any minute now and . . . . there they are!"

Extended across the highway ahead, blocking traffic in both directions, stood a single line of citizens of all ages, all wearing bright t-shirts with the words, "FREEDOM FOR KANE," emblazoned across their chests. Their arms were locked to indicate they would not allow anyone to pass and in their hands they clutched tight to the leashes of their dogs, dogs of all sizes and breeds which stood in front of them, barking and wagging their tails in excitement. Stretched horizontally in the very center of their line lay a colossal St Bernard, spread out on his back as if to convey the message; "No one shall pass."

As Nick's car approached, several people moved aside with their dogs to allow just enough room for him to pass, waving him through with friendly cheers. As his car blew past, rounding a hillside corner and out of sight, the passageway through the line was quickly resealed, arms once again interlocked.

This was the scene that greeted the body of police cars that were now forced to come to a standstill or risk injuring several pedestrians and dogs. The two sides remained, unmoving for several moments before Captain Moreno called out to the pedestrians through a loudspeaker mounted on his vehicle and instructed them to allow law enforcement to pass.

"We will let you pass," yelled back a heavily bearded man before nodding to his comrades, "in a few short minutes."

With that, everyone in the line, arms still locked, sat down in the road.

Moreno stepped out of his vehicle and with several of his men, walked toward the line. As they approached, they were greeted by the many dozens of dogs on the line with various barks, growls, howls, baying and yips. The St Bernard still stretched out on his back, cautioned the officers with a very deep throated "WOOF!"

Moreno sighed deeply before issuing instructions to a sergeant standing nearby, ordering him to relay information of their situation and instructing the police helicopter to maintain a visual on the suspect. He further issued an order to all police who might be on the road ahead to be on the lookout for the fleeing vehicle.

Turning back to the cacophony of dog noises directed toward him he could only shake his head and laugh.

Not far ahead of the protest scene, Nick's car had rounded another curve in the highway as he continued his escape. Pulling back the ceiling covering to reveal a sun-roof, he could see the helicopters overhead.

"Now comes the real trick," he announced to Kane.

Looming ahead on the highway stood a large tunnel which permitted traffic to pass through a sizable mountain that stretched across the highway's path.

"Get ready to get out of the car when I tell you," Nick said to Kane. "You're going to have to move quickly. Do exactly as say."

Kane cocked his head to the side, questioning the next move.

The four-lane highway that passed through the tunnel was lightly traveled on that day, and Nick turned on his car's headlights as they entered, squinting his eyes, forcing them to adjust to the darkness of the passage. It didn't take him long to spot what his eyes were searching for.

"There it is!" he exclaimed.

Parked by the curb of the road ahead, its emergency lights blinking, sat a mid-sized SUV. Nick hurriedly pulled up behind it and came to a stop. Shifting his car into the "park" position but leaving his engine running, he assured himself no other vehicles were passing, and he opened his door and yelled out for Kane to follow him. The dog scrambled to comply.

They were greeted by a man with a build and look similar to Nick's, who sported an identical shirt, loudly decorated with Hawaiian floral. He was accompanied by a sable collie.

The two men exchanged greetings as the stranger, and his dog jumped into the front seat of Nick's car. Kane couldn't help but notice as the collie passed closely by him that it was a female and he stopped for a moment, watching her as she assumed his former seat on the passenger's side.

Waiting for a break in the traffic that whizzed by them in the center lane, the stranger pulled away from the curb and headed toward the tunnel exit. The passenger's side window was rolled down, and the female collie stuck her head out looking back at Kane as they drove away. Kane returned her gaze longingly.

As the car sped from view, Kane hadn't noticed Nick was holding open the door to the SUV, waiting for him to enter.

"Oh come on," Nick chided Kane as he noticed where his attention was focused. "There'll be plenty of time for that later. Come on, you lady killer, you!"

Nick laughed as Kane jumped into the car and assumed a spot in the front passenger seat. Reaching in the back seat Nick grabbed a shirt that was decorated with a subdued pattern, and after exchanging it for the brightly colored one he was wearing, he cautiously pulled his car into traffic.

As expected, Nick's car was recognized by the helicopters waiting at the other side of the mountain tunnel, and they continued their aerial surveillance, unaware that the collie and the driver in the bright shirt were not the suspects they were seeking.

"You're going to have to stay down for a while, boy," Nick told Kane, following several cars behind. "We don't want anyone to spot you. There's water there in a bowl on the back seat for you. We've still got a drive ahead of us before we can get you to safety and I don't know what to expect."

CHAPTER TWENTY-SIX

May hung up the kitchen phone and called for Elizabeth. Since Kane's run across the bridge, the calls from reporters had begun to pick up again, but this call was special.

"I have incredible news," May told her daughter who came rushing in. "That was Sally on the phone. That man we saw in the car on TV, the one who rescued Kane from the bridge, apparently he's affiliated with John Hadley. Somehow, he and Kane got away from the police, and he's going to meet all of us, at the clinic."

Elizabeth was confused. "But how . . . ."

"They made a switch," May said, breathlessly gathering her purse. "I'll explain it all to you on the way. We have to meet Sally at the clinic. The man, the one who caught Kane, is taking him there so you and Sally can perform the procedure."

"I don't believe it," Elizabeth repeated, grabbing a light jacket from the hall closet. "Who is that man? Did she say?"

"No, she didn't," May replied, pausing as she crossed the den toward the front door, "and here's something strange; the man gave specific instructions to make sure we bring Ben with us."

Elizabeth rushed to fetch Ben from the backyard, but when she returned with him, she found her mother standing in the doorway looking with trepidation toward the highway.

"It's them," she uttered angrily under her breath, "those people, spying on us from the car over there on the road."

"They're back?" Elizabeth said, moving next to May. "Those creeps, those spies from Prometheacorp?"

They stared in silent anger at the dark SUV parked just outside the gate.

"They must know Kane will try to make his way back to us," May concluded. "They're watching our every move. If we drive to the clinic, they'll follow us and catch him."

May turned away from the doorway as an idea occurred to her.

"I know how to get rid of them," She declared. Fishing through her purse she located a business card and reaching for the telephone, she quickly dialed the number she found on it. While she waited for her call to be answered, she instructed Elizabeth to take Ben to the car and to be prepared to leave.

Twenty minutes later as dusk approached, the two hired hands in the car at the gate were fighting monotony and having difficulty staying awake. They were unaware of the police car that had just pulled up behind them and just as oblivious to the policeman who approached them on the driver's side of their vehicle. His loud tap on their window, unexpected as it was, startled them from their lethargy and they both swore aloud.

Sergeant Goodwin indicated for the driver to lower his window and the driver complied. Taking his time, the sergeant looked carefully at both men and then peered over their shoulders into the back seat.

"Evening, gentlemen," Goodwin greeted them.

"Have we done something wrong, Sergeant?" the driver asked innocently.

Sergeant Goodwin slowly began asking questions as to the reason they were parked beside the road, what was their destination and other routine inquiries. As the driver explained that they had grown tired and had decided to rest, he was dismayed to see May drive her car through the gate and onto the highway. Elizabeth sat next to her in front and Ben sat silently in the back seat.

The driver anxiously interrupted his interrogation, reaching for his ignition key. "You know what, Sergeant? We're all rested now, and I think we'll be fine, so we'll just be on our way."

"Hold on," Sergeant Goodwin stopped him. "Let me see your registration and insurance, sir."

Seething with anger and frustration, the driver rustled through the glove box and withdrew the certificates.

The sergeant unhurriedly read the information he was handed before instructing the driver to wait while he verified the details on the computer in his vehicle. Glancing in the direction May had driven, he smiled as he casually walked back to his car. The driver of the SUV angrily banged his fist on his steering wheel.

The sun was setting, and lights on the businesses located along the mountain road Nick was driving were just being illuminated. Glancing in his rearview mirror, he could see Kane, resting uneasily on the back seat. His eyes had never closed during the long drive which had been made longer by Nick's decision to travel back roads rather than main highways in an effort to avoid detection. It also gave them access to hidden roadside stops where Nick could allow Kane out of the car momentarily to relieve himself.

"We should be arriving at our destination in about half an hour, my friend," Nick called out to Kane. "I'll let you in on a secret. I think we've found a way that will allow you to stay

with Ben. I can't give you all the details just now, but . . . ."
He held up a hand, his fingers crossed.

Kane sat up and barked cheerfully.

"Now," Nick said, suddenly turning serious. "We're still okay on fuel. Only problem is, I'm going to need to find a restroom soon. I'm not going to be able to hold out for another half hour."

Kane cocked his head.

"Yeah, I know," Nick said with a nod. "The whole world is *your* bathroom, but I'm a little more inhibited than you. Its got to be a clean restroom or not at all. And I think I may have found the relief I seek just ahead."

Standing by itself beside the road, a lone gas station came into view, its brightly illuminated signs advertising gasoline and food items which Nick knew would be far less appetizing in person than they were pictured.

"I'm sure hungry, but not *that* hungry," he muttered as he eyed the graphic of an opulently prepared burrito. "Just give me a couple minutes in a nice, comfortable comfort station, and we'll be out of here."

Nick slowly pulled his car into one of two designated parking spaces in front of the convenience store adjacent to the gasoline pumps. Turning off the engine, he surveyed the area to ensure that there was no one else around before getting out of the car and opening the back door. Leaning in, he looked into the cargo area located behind the back seat.

"Damn!" he exclaimed. "No blankets. Nothing to cover you up with until I get back. Okay, listen. Get down on the floor there and don't move, OK? No one should be able to see you there, and I'll lock the doors. I'll be super quick, I promise."

Complying with Nick's order, Kane huddled on the floor by the back seat. Satisfied, Nick closed and locked the doors to the car. He made one more cursory look around the station to assure himself that they were alone before hustling into the store. Inside, the store clerk directed Nick toward the restrooms located at the back.

It happened that early evening was the time the Keegan brothers finally managed to get out of bed and start their day and on this particular evening, they were on their way to the home of one of their disreputable friends to indulge in a full night of drinking and illegally pirated cable football. They were already intoxicated well above the legal limit and had run short of beer, recently acquired under cover of darkness from the liquor store in town. They now figured to replenish their inventory as they directed their car into the space next to the SUV parked in front of the roadside station they passed along their route.

Kane lifted his head in alarm as the deep thud of the stereo drew near. He knew that sound.

As Mitch cut the engine of his vehicle and it sputtered into eventual silence, the two brothers rummaged through a paper sack they pulled from the glove box. Fishing out various credit cards they eventually located one they agreed might actually work, and Conrad was assigned the task of getting the goods while Mitch remained behind the wheel. Throwing his weight against the door, it took Conrad three attempts before it finally swung wide, hitting the side of the SUV parked next to it with a very loud thud.

"Oops!" he giggled, sliding from the seat.

Closing the creaking door of his car, he glanced into the SUV, knocking on the window and yelling out, "Sorry!" in case anyone happened to be sitting inside. He didn't see anyone, but through the tinted back window, he did spot something that seized his attention.

Thinking at first he may have glimpsed a white fox coat on the back seat floor that might if acquired, offer a generous return, Conrad positioned his hands in a circle on the window to shadow the reflective glare of the bright signage nearby. Placing his face against the glass and peering through the shading offered by his hands, he swore in surprise when he was finally able to figure out what was actually inside.

Conrad grabbed the handle of his car and gave it a fierce tug, placing his left foot beside the door for leverage. After several attempts, the door grated open, and he jumped inside, breathing heavily as he slammed it behind him.

"You're not going to believe this, man," Conrad said to his brother, trying to catch his breath. "Remember what they were talking about last night over at Bert's place, that dog that's worth almost a quarter million dollars, that dog that they took away from the retard? I just seen him! I swear!"

Mitch was skeptical. "Naw," he said impatiently. "How d'ya know?"

Suddenly Nick rushed out of the store. Unlocking the SUV, he jumped behind the wheel, started the engine, pulled out of the parking space and onto the road.

"That's him!" Mitch exclaimed. "They had his picture on the TV. That's the guy that snatched the dog off the Golden Gate Bridge!"

Forever Stay

As he watched the SUV drive away, Mitch was struck with a sudden inspiration. "You know what? That guy's wanted by the cops for kidnapping that dog. You know what we're gonna do? We're gonna get that guy, turn him over to the cops and collect the reward money for the dog."

Conrad was alive with excitement. "Shit, man! Can you imagine the look on those cops' faces when we walk into that station? All these years they've been on our ass, and we turn out to be heroes. How 'bout that!"

With an empty bladder and a mission very nearly accomplished, a satisfying sensation of comfort settled over Nick as he guided his car along the mountain road that would soon intersect with the highway that would deliver him and Kane to the veterinary clinic.

Kane however, was far from any such feeling. From the back seat, he watched through the window. His senses were telling him that trouble would soon be trailing them. Seeing the reflection of Kane's discomfort from the rearview mirror, Nick thought to reassure him.

"What?" Nick asked. "Are you worried about those two clowns in the car back at the station? Relax, boy! They were far too plastered to notice us."

Kane was not reassured, and his wariness soon gave way to distress as the headlights of the Keegan brothers' car came into view some distance behind them. Nick tensed as he, too, caught sight of it.

"You think?" Nick asked Kane. "Maybe they just happen to be going the same way as us. It happens."

Kane's gaze remained on the approaching vehicle.

"Yeah," Nick admitted, "I'm not too comfortable about this either. Maybe we better not take a chance."

Rounding a mountain curve, Nick spotted a small dirt road leading into the trees that lined the route. Quickly turning his vehicle onto the dusty path, he disregarded a handmade posting that read, "PRIVATE ROAD. NO TRESPASSING."

The crude roadway was heavily rutted with deep creases created by rains past and Nick promptly decelerated to accommodate the harshness of the route. After traveling at a snail's pace for a minute, he stopped the car and turned off his headlights. In the silence, he listened with Kane for any sound that might tell them if they were being followed, but all they heard was the sound of the fine sand they had thrown up from the road as it returned to earth to light on the SUV.

When no sound of approaching danger could be heard, Nick breathed easier.

"See?" he comforted Kane. "False alarm. Now, let's see if I can get this thing turned around."

No sooner had these words been spoken than the noisy sound of a car engine accompanied by the unnerving racket of an over-amplified bass suddenly pierced the silence, the combined bedlam leaving no doubt as to who was coming. The clamor was approaching at an alarming speed, and it was only moments before headlights, filtered through the settling dust, could be seen drawing ever closer.

Taking little time to react, Nick quickly started the engine of the SUV and accelerated forward hoping that his vehicle would be in better shape to withstand the hazards of the roadway than the car advancing on them. Kane was tossed to and fro in the back seat as Nick did his best to outrun his pursuers while trying to steer the SUV along the ruinous roadway.

The pursuit was not a lengthy one. He was forced to brake for a closed wooden gate that spanned the road. Centered on the gate was a large metal sign emphatically warning, "NO TRESPASSING."

For a moment, but only for a moment, Nick considered smashing through the gate, but when all was weighed, he opted instead to attempt turning around and to run a course around the Keegans, hoping he could outrun them before they could turn around themselves. He was not willing to risk invoking the wrath of the property owner on the other side of the gate nor was he confident that the SUV he was driving could break through the gate with enough speed and force to knock it from its hinges.

It was the wrong decision.

In his attempt to turn the vehicle he immediately ran into a large bush that would not yield, and when he shoved the gear shift into reverse, he was met with a large tree at his rear. Between the two obstacles, any hope of a speedy withdrawal was quickly dashed. Like a novice driver learning to park parallel for the first time, he was repeatedly moving to and fro, all the while making no progress. The Keegans brought their car to a stop very near, and Mitch casually stepped out, eventually followed by his brother who first had to wrestle open the consistently jammed passenger door. Nick was still hopelessly attempting to free the SUV as they approached, and they giggled at his pathetic attempt.

"Hey!" Conrad shouted, banging on the door of the SUV with the ever-present baseball bat he had remembered to retrieve from his car. "Need some help?"

Nick stopped his vehicle, and the engine automatically died. He clutched the steering wheel for a moment, catching his breath before instructing Kane to remain where he was. "I'll talk to them," he told him. After a deep breath, he opened his door and faced the two unkempt men standing beside the SUV. He neglected to close the door behind him.

"Looks like you and your collie dog there got yourself stuck, don't it?" Mitch said with a smile.

"What?" Nick replied nervously. Gesturing toward Kane, he corrected Mitch, "Oh, you mean Lassie? Yeah, she gets nervous when I'm out late at night like this. I hate driving at night, don't you? So we got lost, and I thought I'd stop and get directions because my GPS is acting up but, well, as you can see there's a 'No Trespassing' sign, so . . . ."

"Couldn't the guy at the store back there help you out?" Mitch asked, scratching his head.

"Him?" Nick asked, pointing up the road. "No. Useless. I don't think he's even from around here."

"Know what I think?" asked Conrad, nervously fidgeting with his bat. "I'll be right up front with you. See, we knew you drove up this way to try and get away from us, but we knew you cut off this way 'cause of all the dust you was kickin' up. Now *you* know that *we* know you're trying to get away with that valuable dog you got in the back seat there." He emphasized his suspicion by firmly pushing on Nick's chest with the tip of the bat to accentuate his words.

"Look, I told you," Nick countered, "the dog's name is Lassie and will you please stop touching me with that bat. Now if you'll back your truck up, I'll . . . ."

"I'll tell you what we're going to do," Mitch interrupted, holding up a hand. "We're gonna move that dog over to our car and then how 'bout you just follow us over to the police station not much further down the road. That sound like a plan?"

"Conrad, get the dog," Mitch said, nodding toward the SUV.

Conrad brushed past Nick, nearly knocking him to his feet.

"Hold on there!" Nick yelled, grabbing him by the back Nick of the shoulders. Wheeling around quickly, Conrad hit Nick on his jaw with the back of his clenched fist, sending him sprawling to the ground.

"Don't you *ever* touch me!" Conrad yelled.

"Okay," Nick managed to say as he pulled his cell phone from his pocket while he pulled himself to his feet. Standing unsteadily, he wiped a trickle of blood that was running from the corner of his mouth and started to dial a number on his phone. His attempt was immediately stopped as the thick part of Conrad's bat came crashing down on his hand, knocking the phone to the ground.

Wincing in pain, Nick watched as Conrad proceeded to smash the phone with several blows from his bat. Nick thoughtlessly grabbed his arm, attempting to stop him and was pushed back with an animal growl from his assailant. The push back was immediately followed by a blow to the side of the head from Conrad's bat and Nick fell to the ground, unconscious and bleeding.

"Conrad, hold on!" Mitch shouted.

Thoroughly infuriated, Conrad loomed over the fallen man. "I just told him never to touch me! Now I'm gonna have to make sure he don't forget!" he yelled, raising his bat over his head to deliver another blow.

Mitch started to say a few words of discouragement to his brother but was stopped before any sound could come from his throat.

Wielding the bat high over his head as he prepared to strike, the attacker suddenly felt the claws of an unseen savage creature as they tore into his back while simultaneously, with ferocious strength, his right forearm was pierced and torn by fangs of fury.

Screaming, Conrad dropped his bat and spun around wildly in an attempt to dislodge the fiend on his back.

"Get him off! Get him off!" he shrieked.

Kane's jaws gripped his enemy's wrist with unyielding force. He shook his head for extra measure to elicit maximum pain.

While he watched Conrad wrestling with the dog, Mitch was torn between saving himself and saving his brother. When he spotted the bat that had been inadvertently dropped to the ground, the decision was made for him.

Leaping forward and grabbing the instrument in one swift move, he clenched the handle of the bat tightly and with a mighty swing struck the collie on the side of the neck just slightly below his skull. The action had its desired effect, and the blow elicited a short, terrible cry from the dog as he was knocked to the ground, ripping a choice piece of flesh from his adversary's wrist in the process.

Kane remained on the ground where he landed, not moving and making no sound.

"We screwed it up!" Mitch cried. "We were gonna be heroes, and now it's all screwed up! They'll probably lock us up for assault, and they won't give us any reward for a dead dog!"

Conrad, jumping up and down, screamed even louder as he swore and clutched his arm.

"I'm bleeding!" he shrieked. "Get me to a doctor! I'm going to bleed to death!"

Overflowing with anger, he punctuated his agonized screams with a sickening kick to Kane's side.

Dropping the bat to the ground, Mitch ripped off his soiled shirt and attempted to form a tourniquet around his brother's bleeding wrist.

"That won't do no good!" Conrad howled, pushing Mitch away. "Get me to an emergency room! Quick! I'm dyin' here!"

As he turned to deliver another fierce kick to Kane's inert form, the two men were suddenly startled by the glare of headlights aimed in their direction from the other side of the gate as a large double-cab pickup came to a stop.

"We gotta get out of here!" Mitch shouted, grabbing his brother.

After the customary battle with the reluctant passenger door of the car, he pushed Conrad inside and ran around to the driver's side, sliding into the seat. His attempt to start the car's motor was met with some resistance and not until a tall, mustached, elderly man in a worn cowboy hat swung wide the gate and walked in their direction did the car's engine finally agree to turn over. Grinding the gearshift into reverse, Mitch, with sloppy steering, guided his car backward down the dusty road from which he had arrived.

The headlights from the stranger's truck revealed two bleeding figures lying by the road. Rushing to Nick, he knelt beside him and touched the artery in his neck.

"Hey there, friend," he said softly, gently shaking Nick's shoulder. "You still with us? I heard the racket and saw the lights from my place up yonder."

Opening his eyes, Nick stared uncomprehendingly into the man's face, dazed and disoriented.

"We better get you looked after. You think you can make it to my truck?" the man asked.

Suddenly remembering what had just transpired, Nicks eyes focused as he pushed himself from the man's hold on him and began looking desperately around.

"Where's Kane? Did they take him?" he managed to ask, panic rising in his voice.

"Kane?" the man asked. "You lookin' for the collie dog over there? That dog saved your life from what I saw."

Nick spotted Kane's form nearby, lying quiet and still.

"Oh, Kane!" he groaned, and with difficulty, he managed to pull himself to the collie's side, tears filling his eyes.

"I'm sorry I couldn't protect you, my sweet friend," he said, his voice choking with sadness. "And you risked your life to save *me*."

As Nick wept beside Kane, stroking his fur, the stranger approached and, dropping to one knee he began checking the dog over, looking at his eyes and in his mouth and then feeling his ribs.

"I got good news for you," the stranger said. "He's alive. I work a lot with dogs on my ranch here, and I'm willin' to bet he might even make it through if we can get him to a vet quick."

"Oh, thank god!" Nick exclaimed through his tears. "I need to get him to the Los Olvera Vet Clinic about twenty minutes away from here. They're waiting for him right now. Please! I'll pay you whatever you ask if you'll drive us there right now."

"We got to get you to the emergency room first, friend, then we can tend to the dog," the man said.

"Absolutely not!" Nick declared, pulling himself to his feet with some effort. "First the dog, then me. I insist! Please! I beg you! You don't know what I've gone through to get him this far. You don't know what *he's* gone through."

The man stood, beating at the dust on his knee with his hat. "Actually, I think I do," he said with some solemnity.

Nick braced himself.

"I know who you are and I know who this dog is," the man told him. "You can't turn on the TV without some mention of the two of you fugitives."

"Look," Nick said fearfully. "I'm trying to get this dog back to his family. We think we've figured out a way they'll be able to keep him, but I've got to get him there before anyone else can grab him for the reward. All I'm asking is . . . ."

241

"Hold on," the man said with a chuckle as he offered his hand. "My name's Billy Galbert. If you'll let me, I'd like nothin' better than to help you get this dog back to that little boy. But you need to see a doctor first."

Nick could hardly retain himself as he grabbed his new friend's hand and shook it vigorously, disregarding the pain he felt in his hand that was the result of the blow he received from Conrad.

"Please," Nick gushed through a rain of grateful tears. "We've got to take care of him first."

"Well," said Galbert, "Judging from the strength in your handshake I guess you'll be okay for a while."

Grabbing a rumpled leather glove from his hip pocket, he placed it on his hand and picked up the bloodied bat, tossing it into the bed of his pickup.

"Fingerprints," he informed Nick as he removed the glove. "Now, let's get this vehicle of yours out of the road so we can get this fella some help."

CHAPTER TWENTY-SEVEN

Sally carefully examined and evaluated Kane's wounds as he lay on a table in the veterinary clinic surgery, an IV tube connected to his leg. He had gained consciousness and was now panting heavily after receiving an injection to ease his pain and Nick, and Galbert stood nearby, ready to offer help if needed.

Leaning over the dog's face, Sally spoke softly to him as she scratched behind his ear. "You're going to be fine, my boy. A lesser dog might have faced a tougher recovery, but I know you. I know the promise you made to my brother before he died and I know that you'll keep that promise to take care of his grandson if it takes every ounce of your strength and willpower to do it."

Turning to the two men standing nearby, she directed her remarks to them. "Looks like you got him here just in time. If that idiot's aim had been just slightly higher, his skull would have been crushed."

"Well," said Galbert as he placed his hat on his head, "we better get this boy here over to the doctor so he can get checked out."

"Look, you've done more than anyone could ask of you," Nick responded. "Our friends are going to be here in a few minutes, and I can get one of them to run me over to the emergency room. But I can't thank you enough. You saved me, you saved Kane, and you may have even saved Ben."

"Then I guess I'll drop by police headquarters in the morning after you've had time to retrieve your vehicle from my place," Galbert said with a nod. "Between the fingerprints on that bat and my eyewitness account, I figure the Keegan brothers have a long stretch in jail to look forward to. So for now, I guess you can just call me The Lone Ranger as I ride off into the distance."

He touched the brim of his hat with his index finger and walked out the back door.

Soon after his departure, Nick and Sally heard a knock on the front door of the clinic. Sally handed Nick a set of keys and sent him to answer as she busied herself treating Kane's injuries.

At the front door, Nick peeked through the blinds that had been drawn closed before admitting May, Ben, and Elizabeth.

"What are you . . . . What happened?" Elizabeth stammered in confusion.

"I'll explain it all to you later," Nick said, calming her. "Kane was injured on the way here, but he's going to be fine. Sally's treating him right now."

"Oh, my god!" May exclaimed as she headed toward the surgery.

"Wait," Nick said, grabbing her arm gently. "We need to get Ben's approval before the procedure."

"What?" May asked. "Why would he possibly object? He's regressed since you saw him last, and he's not old enough to . . . ."

"I think he is," Nick interrupted. "Everyone has been making decisions about his life and about Kane. Don't you think it's time for Ben and Kane to make their own decisions now?"

Elizabeth and her mother turned to look at Ben. He had seated himself on the waiting room couch and had remained there, quite still, his hands relaxed on his knees, staring ahead with an expression of curiosity. May seated herself next to him. She made no attempt to put her arm around him or to cuddle him because she knew he would only push her away.

"Is Kane here?" Ben asked.

"Yes, Ben, he is," May replied. "He's with Great Aunt Sally in the next room, but we need to leave him with her for a while so she can help him rest."

"Is he going to go away again?" Ben asked.

"Maybe not," his mother said. "We don't know for sure, but listen to me, Ben. Elizabeth and Great Aunt Sally think they know a way to fix Kane so the big company that took him away from you won't want him anymore. If it works, he'll probably get to live with us again but listen, sweetheart. You know Kane is . . . ."

"Kane is the greatest dog in the world," Ben said, looking in his mother's direction but still not making eye contact. "He's the smartest and . . . ."

"Yes," that's right, May interrupted. "He's unlike any other dog in the world. But what if . . . What if he was just like every other dog in the world? What if he wasn't so extra special smart anymore? Wouldn't you still love him as much as you always have?"

"Is Great Aunt Sally going to make him, so he's not as smart anymore?" he asked, his voice increasing in volume and concern.

"Well," his mother responded, continuing to speak in soft tones, "to those of us who love Kane, he would still be extra special except he'll be, well, just like other dogs."

"Great Aunt Sally is going to make him like that?" Ben yelled back at her.

"Only if you tell her it's okay," Elizabeth interjected. "It's your decision to make, Ben."

Jumping from the couch, Ben started walking swiftly in all directions. Heading toward a wall, he would swiftly turn and walk toward the sofa, then toward another wall before changing direction again, all the while exhibiting signs of extreme anxiety, tapping his fingers vigorously on his pant leg.

"This was wrong," May declared. "He's not old enough to understand. We shouldn't put this burden on him. He's not old enough to make this decision."

Elizabeth sat next to her mother and placed her arm around her shoulder. "Mom," she began in an effort to console her.

Ben was growing more frantic as he rushed about the room. In such situations, the family knew better than to attempt to restrain or comfort him as he would only become even more agitated.

After watching his behavior for several minutes, Elizabeth finally stood. "I'd better go in," she announced and started toward the surgery door.

"Wait," Nick said, stopping her. He watched Ben for just a moment longer before approaching him and kneeling down on one knee.

"Ben," he called out in a normal, conversational voice.

The boy continued his erratic behavior for a moment before very suddenly coming to a halt near Nick. Though he continued tapping his leg, he turned his head in Nick's direction.

"What happened to your face?" Ben asked.

"Oh, that?" Nick replied, lightly touching the bloody spot on his head. "I met up with some men who didn't want me to bring Kane back here to be with you. But you know what? Kane stopped them. He wouldn't let them hurt me anymore because he knew how important it was for me to get him back to you because more than anything else, he wants to be with you for the rest of his life."

Ben thought about it for a moment before asking, "For the rest of his life?"

"That's right," Elizabeth joined in as she kneeled next to Nick.

Still tapping his leg, Ben looked at the wall, buried deep in thought.

"Will Kane still know me if Great Aunt Sally fixes him?" Ben finally asked.

"I think so," Elizabeth replied. "I hope so. We'll have to see."

"And those other people," Ben asked, "they won't want him anymore?"

"We hope not," Nick answered.

Ben remained deep in thought.

"So you have to ask yourself," Nick said, "would it be so bad if Kane was just like any other dog? If you ask my opinion, maybe that isn't so bad because even a regular dog is still something very, very special. But that's your decision to make. Nobody here is trying to tell you what to do, and we all believe you're a big enough person to decide for yourself what's best."

Suddenly Ben stopped tapping. Looking first in Nick and Elizabeth's direction and then toward his mother he announced, "I think he should be a regular dog and live with me the rest of his life."

Elated, May and Elizabeth stood, resisting the impulse to hug him. Nick, still kneeling, held his hand up in the air.

"Wait," he said. "One more thing, Ben. Don't you think Kane ought to give his approval first?"

"Nick!" Elizabeth cried out. "What are you . . . ?"

"Yes," Ben replied with an air of finality.

Nick nodded to Ben and stood then nodded again, this time toward the boy's sister.

Elizabeth led the way down the hallway to the surgery door followed by the others. As the door was swung open revealing Kane lying flat on the surgery table, Ben paused before proceeding.

Kane was lying very still, no longer panting, feeling no pain. At first, Ben touched a bandage that had been applied to Kane's neck and then his hand moved to stroke the bottom of the dog's muzzle. Kane's tail thumped against the table very slowly. Placing his face close to the collie, Ben spoke to him softly.

"Kane," Ben began, "I'm glad you came back to me. I missed you more than you'll ever know. I guess you probably missed me too or you wouldn't have tried so hard to get back to me. I'm really glad you did because I need you to be with me the rest of my life. They want to do something to you that will keep those bad men away from us so you can keep living with me but when they do this thing it's going to make you different, so you'll be just like all the other dogs. I don't know if that's a good thing, but if we have each other, maybe it doesn't matter because I'm going to love you no matter what."

Kane managed to lick Ben's nose.

"Kane says it's okay to go ahead," Ben said, looking in Sally's direction.

Looking back at the collie, Ben said to him, "I don't want you ever to leave me again Kane, because I really, really need you. I want us always to stay together. Forever."

With that, Ben turned and walked from the room and only stopped when he reached the hallway outside. He could still see Kane until Elizabeth closed the door. Kane was looking back at him, his tail gently thumping on the table.

CHAPTER TWENTY-EIGHT

When Sally telephoned the executive offices of Prometheacorp to inform them the microchip that had been embedded in Kane had been deactivated, she was met with silence by the executives who had assembled around Tom Burch's desk to join in the conference call. Burch asked for and received permission from Sally to dispatch one of his researchers to confirm her claim and then ended the call with an abrupt statement that he would discuss the implications of the news with his corporate attorneys. It would come as no surprise to him that he wouldn't be in a position to discuss the corporation's business with anyone for much longer.

In the several years, Burch served as CEO, he only had about two or three meetings with his Chairman of the Board, an elderly individual named Donald Shapiro, the acknowledged power behind the corporation. Shapiro's policy was to remain hands off of the day to day operations and tended to make an appearance only when it pertained to matters of major importance. The firing of Thomas Burch was one such occasion, and now he sat, removed from the others, silently watching through thick, tinted eyeglasses from the back of the room, both hands clutching his walking cane in front of him.

After the disaster that was the shareholders meeting and the subsequent spectacle involving the dog's escape across the Golden Gate Bridge, the corporation's share values plunged to a level rarely seen in the history of Wall Street. Though Burch continued to promise that shares would go through the roof once the dog was captured and all of the details pertaining to the Mastermind Program were safely and secretly locked away in the corporate vaults, all respect had vanished for the CEO and even those who stood to lose on their hefty investments turned all their sympathy toward the collie that got away.

With the news that the dog was now worthless and that the secret was lost, probably forever, the whole existence of Prometheacorp was in question and so, after waving everyone else from the room, Shapiro informed Burch that his services were no longer needed. Burch made a feeble attempt to explain how his plan was to keep news of the microchip deactivation quiet and to hint to the public that the Mastermind Program was proceeding ahead as planned. If they could keep that news active long enough for the value of shares to rise again, he hastily told Shapiro, the two of them could dump their shares before the truth came out. Meanwhile, they would engender goodwill by generously donating the dog back to the kid and even form a foundation to help train and supply dogs to other autistic children.

He was stopped short by the Chairman of the Board who quite simply told him, "Get out."

Thomas Burch would have received a two hundred fifty million dollar severance package in cash and stock but since Prometheacorp was thrown into bankruptcy and the stock was now worthless, it would take considerable time and costly attorneys for the former CEO to mount a lawsuit, one that would ultimately leave him with far less capital than he would have had if he had simply stepped away from the table.

One day he realized that he couldn't even remember the name of the collie that had brought about his downfall.

Thanks to the eyewitness testimony of Billy Galbert, the Keegan brothers were convicted of assault,battery, attempted theft, parole violation and various and sundried other charges all of which added up to sentences lasting several years. The damage to Conrad's arm, which was the result of a nasty dog bite, continued to generate pain for many years after his prison sentence had been served.

The demise of Prometheacorp spared Nick Stanley the indignity of being prosecuted and fired from the company he had betrayed since there was no job to which he could return and no legal staff to mount a case. The public at large was overwhelmingly supportive of his heroic rescue on the Golden Gate Bridge in the face of overwhelming odds making prosecution difficult. Ultimately a plea deal was struck in which he was convicted of refusing to stop for a police officer, and he was sentenced to six months community service, said service to be spent working at the local animal shelter. His notoriety brought him to the attention of many animal rights organizations from which he fielded a copious number of job offers. When he finally found time to take care of a pet, he adopted the small Shetland Sheepdog that Thomas Burch and his associates had at one time intended to present to Ben. He named the puppy Citizen, a not so veiled tribute to a certain collie with whom Nick's name was now linked.

Public school was soon in session, and May resumed her teaching career receiving accolades not only for the excellent work she did with her sixth-grade students but also for her dedication and her ability to improve the reading skills of all the young people for whom she was responsible. She was able to lease the vineyards on the McLaughlin property to a neighboring winery who, in exchange, installed a water-efficient irrigation system that could be used by her husband when he returned from his foreign job assignment when the winery's lease expired. May was optimistic that a new beginning with Paul might be possible.

Sally found herself more in demand at the veterinary clinic than ever. As a mentor to several young people, she found little opportunity for retirement though she always managed to carve out time to spend with family.

Elizabeth resumed her studies at the university and distinguished herself in all of her subjects. During school breaks, she worked with her Great Aunt Sally at the clinic. She tried with some success to forgive Nick for the dishonesty of which he was initially guilty and although they resumed a cautious relationship, time and distance was not conducive to the cultivation of any meaningful romantic attachment. They remained good friends.

Ben, by jumps and starts, made tremendous progress in learning to overcome the great mental and behavioral challenges life laid before him. Doctors determined that, like many with autism spectrum disorder, his intelligence was quite advanced and those around him never surrendered their hope that one day they would understand the very unique way Ben's thought process worked. Though he did not often speak and think with the maturity he exhibited that night in Sally's clinic he would sometimes, without warning, surprise everyone around him with observations that were quite profound. The school at which his mother taught was able to provide him with special classes to which he was allowed to bring his assistance dog. The dog never left his side.

Sally, May, and Elizabeth and, from a distance, Paul, could not imagine a life without Kane.

Autumn was punctual that year despite the pervasive California drought that now seemed to be the new normal. The continually warm weather confused the trees and plant life in the Northern California mountains, driving the wildlife from the safety of their camouflage to the danger of rural civilization which was constantly expanding. Along the mountain path, Kane had once walked with Sam Crisp the colors were quickly changing in an attempt to catch up with the season.

One bright Sunday morning early that autumn Kane again walked along that familiar path, several steps ahead of his beloved family. Small drops of water collected on the leaves of the trees, the result of a very rare and brief rain that had occurred the night before and all the pleasures he had known in days past flooded his memory with both melancholy and solace as he sniffed every fallen leaf and every flower along the way. On such a day even the lingering pain that resulted from the attack he had recently experienced was forgotten.

Suddenly he stopped. A sound, a smell, a movement in the distance along the path before him, *something* was telling him that his old friend Sam was just ahead, calling him to walk by his side.

Quickly turning, the collie rushed back to his family, seeking their permission to race ahead. Sally, May, Elizabeth, and Ben walked arm in arm, and they recognized in his expression the permission he was seeking.

"Go ahead, boy," Elizabeth said with a smile, motioning him forward. "We'll catch up."

With an unbounded joy, Kane whirled around, leaped ahead down the trail and ran promptly out of sight.

Flying along the path with a sense of freedom and happiness he had not enjoyed since puppyhood, he sent squirrels and rabbits scampering for cover and startled birds from their perches as he jumped over fallen branches and splashed through small puddles of quickly drying water. He felt he could run like that forever.

Barely one-half mile into his joyous scamper, he stopped quite suddenly and quite still as that certain *something* that had caught his attention a few moments earlier once again overwhelmed his senses. Walking back a few steps along the path he had just run, he was drawn toward a simple tree that had fallen many years ago which lay unnoticed by the trail. It was covered in moss and was suffering the ravages of time and insect infestation, but there it remained, an old, silent, steadfast friend that invited Kane to come closer. His heart was filled with warmth and affection as he recognized that this was the same log on which Sam had often rested not so very long ago while he gently stroked Kane's fur as the two of them shared a quiet, tranquil moment of peace and love. Upon that log, they thanked whatever gods may be for the life they had been given to share with each other.

Kane approached his old friend and sniffed along the bark that still remained, savoring the fragrances that were slowly fading with the aged, decaying wood from which they originated. And there, he was certain, he sensed in a way that only dogs can, the presence of the old man he loved, still seated on the trunk of the dilapidated, decaying tree.

When his family finally caught up with Kane a short while later, they found him lying in that very spot at the side of the fallen tree, curled up like a fox, dozing, untroubled, tranquil, and at peace, dreaming of this place and halcyon days gone by. They remained for a while just watching and allowing him his moment of serenity a bit longer. Soon Ben joined him. Sitting beside his dog, he gently stroked the collie's head.

"Come on, Kane," Ben said softly after several minutes more. "Remember? We're going to say goodbye to Grandpa."

Kane lifted his head and very gently licked the cheek of his boy, and when Ben stood, he did the same, shaking his fur and wagging his tail before merrily striking out again on the trail, leading his family close behind him.

Since Kane was unburdened of the technological weight that had been implanted within him, his family only noticed one significant change in his demeanor. Though there were small signs that his human-like intellect was perhaps not as sharp as it had once been, he was now a much happier dog than he was when he first came to live with them. He was just a dog now. But as Ben soon came to realize, being "just" a dog was a perfect thing to be.

Not very much farther ahead the path led to a slight clearing at the edge of the mountain and continued on several feet where it eventually terminated upon a large boulder that jutted from the side of the mountain and offered a breathtaking view of the valley below. It was this boulder on which Kane first observed May's car the day she and Ben had driven to fetch him to his new life.

Today Kane walked to the edge of the boulder for one last look, and he was soon joined by his family who stood beside him and appreciated the scenic view the location offered.

May and Elizabeth held tightly to Ben's hands as Sally lowered to the ground a large cloth bag she had brought with her from which she withdrew a ceramic vase. Something had nagged at her conscience since she had defied her brother's request that his ashes be spread along the mountain path and one day she finally decided to give in to her guilt. Having disinterred Sam's urn, she now held it before her, preparing to fulfill his wish.

A gentle breeze swept down from the mountain providing the perfect condition for the ritual about to be performed. Removing the lid, Sally turned to Ben, holding the urn before her.

"I think your grandfather would want you to have this honor, Ben," she said as she handed the object to him.

With a warning to hold the urn tight and to be careful, May and Elizabeth released their grip on Ben's hands allowing him to accept it. Holding it with reverence a moment, he turned to address Kane, who watched him closely.

"Say goodbye to Grandpa, Kane," Ben said.

With great care, he held the urn from him and tipped it slightly, allowing the ashes to pour forth as the wind scattered them into the air above the valley. May, Sally and Elizabeth each said a silent prayer and Kane's farewell bark echoed about the mountain.

When the jar had been emptied, Ben returned it to Sally, and after she had placed it back in the bag, the family stood with their arms held tight around one another as they watched the final trace of Sam's earthly remains fade from view. Then turning away from the valley, they walked back along the path which they had traveled, still holding one another close.

Before they left the clearing, Ben paused and turned to see that Kane was still standing upon the boulder, still watching where the ashes had disappeared.

"Kane! Come!" Ben called out to him.

May placed an arm around Ben's shoulder. She noticed that he didn't resist. "Let's let Kane stay just a bit longer," she told him. "Come on." With that, she led Ben along with the others.

We may never fully understand nor really appreciate the devotion, the joy and, yes, the love a dog brings to us, but there is no improvement we can make on a species that is already perfect. And they give all of this to us by simply being a dog.

Kane remained on his lookout point for several minutes before slowly turning and trotting ahead to walk beside the boy he loved.